Serenity Ranch

JASON A. DENSLEY

Copyright © 2021 Jason Densley

All rights reserved.

ISBN: 9798750356553
Stripling Strong Publications

DEDICATION

I dedicate this book to my mother and father. If there was ever a testament to the power of prayer by parents unwilling to give up on a child, yours stands supreme.

SERENITY RANCH

PROLOGUE

The Kittitas Valley is a 90-minute drive southeast of Seattle over the Cascades Mountains. It is a beautiful valley, hedged between rugged mountains, fertile fields, and sagebrush-covered plains.

Ellensburg, the largest city in the valley, is a college town and a farming community. It is also home to the kind of people who look you in the eye, shake your hand, and take your word—even though you just met.

The Yakima River begins on the eastern side of the Cascades, above Ellensburg, and crawls down the dry, desert canyon toward its namesake. It is not the type of river kayakers flock to because there are no white-water rapids, and it flows at a leisurely pace. It is a peaceful river, and nearby college students drink beer and float between its banks on innertubes in the summer sun.

"The Yak," as it's called, is also the only "blue ribbon" trout stream in Washington State and a mecca for fly fisherman across the great Northwest. Native cutthroat and rainbow trout scour the deeper pools and sheltered coves for invertebrate larvae and insects floating downstream.

Even in the hot summer months, snowmelt from the High Cascades feeds the river, and today the water is high. While the current feels manageable, we know there are hidden dangers below the surface.

My father settles into the flowing water of the Yakima River without making a sound. His senses are keen, and he tests each step before committing his weight to the slippery rocks that cover the riverbed. He lost his footing once before and now takes his time to ensure it doesn't happen again.

My father, Robert Coleman, is the CEO of a major pharmaceutical company. This short vacation will probably be his only chance to get away for the remainder of the year because his company has a new product hitting the market in July. If the stock market analysts are correct, his company will corner the market in health and fitness supplements.

I have great admiration for my father because he thoroughly dedicates himself to whatever he is doing. While he is a successful entrepreneur and a shrewd businessman, this weekend he is just a fly fisherman and our father.

My name is Jake, and my little brother is Nate. Even though I am 16 and Nate just turned 11, we are as close as any two brothers can be.

I also fish, but not as well as my dad. He'll probably catch his limit this morning, and if I'm lucky, I'll have mine sometime before June.

Nate, on the other hand, has no interest in fishing. He is solely interested in rocks and the things that live under them. Today, Nate is exploring the canyon alongside the river. He carries an empty 2-liter plastic bottle to hold the grasshoppers, beetles, and other creepy, crawling things he finds. But, of course, our mother will not allow him to bring any of it into the house. However, to be fair, I should also mention that my dad and I are catch-and-release fishermen for the same reason.

I watch Nate scampering among the rocks and know I should talk to him. We had a minor argument about an hour ago, and I realize now that I was stupid to get so upset with him.

Instead, I ignore the prompting and take another shot at catching a fish. I haven't quite nailed the casting rhythm like my father. He is so dialed in with a flyrod that he can put a fly within inches of where he wants it to land and without making the slightest ripple on the surface of the water. My line is more stubborn—it has not yet learned to do that.

After a couple of attempts at casting, my line usually ends up in a tangle of knots or stuck in a tree. I feel like I spend more time getting knots out of my line than fishing.

"Keep your casting arm straighter," my father says, coaching me from across the river. "Not so much wrist action. Think of your arm as an extension of the rod. If you break your wrist during the cast, you'll end up with knots in your line."

"No *shit*." I laugh under my breath. I've been at this all morning, and my patience is wearing thin.

If there's a good place in this river for a rainbow to hide, my father will find it. He makes a remarkable cast, landing the dry fly just upstream of a large boulder and under a thicket of trees. Then, seconds later, he jerks the flyrod back and sets the hook in the rainbow's mouth. From the way it's fighting him, it's sure to be another keeper.

Inspired by his success, I give it one more cast. I strip some line from the reel and allow the leader—the last 8-foot section of clear line—to float downstream so that I have more line to cast. While watching my father, I noticed a ripple on the surface just below a large tree, but I will have to release it perfectly to get the line under a low-hanging branch.

Just as I'm about to cast, a plastic soda bottle floats by, and I lose my concentration. I hate people who litter, especially in a pristine wilderness environment such as this. All I can do is shake my head. But then I notice the insects crawling inside the bottle.

"Nate!" I scream, scanning the riverbank for my younger brother. "Nate, where are you?"

I try running upstream toward the last place I saw him, but I'm wearing chest waders, and the force of the current pushes me back.

So instead, I change course for the riverbank but slip on the river rocks after only a few steps.

Frigid water rushes into my waders at chest level and takes my breath away. The shock is severe, and it feels like someone is stabbing me in the chest with an icepick. I attempt to get my footing on the slick rocks below, but the water level makes it difficult to gain traction.

Realizing my predicament, I yank the suspenders off my shoulders and try to shimmy out of the waders. I get them down to my knees, but I can't get either foot out of the boots.

Seconds before going into full panic mode, I take a deep breath, tuck at my waist, and reach for my right foot underwater. I wrestle with the boot for several seconds, but all I do is waste my breath and energy. It's no use. I can only pray that my father saw me slip and comes to my rescue.

When I hear a voice through the cold, dark waters, my heart leaps. It is a miracle! He *did* see what happened and is coming to save me.

It is precisely at that moment that I see Nate and the frozen expression of terror on his face underwater. His eyes are as big as silver dollars, and his mouth is open in a perpetual scream. The current has him wedged under a sunken log, just inches below the surface.

Instinctively, I reach for Nate, but he and the log are quickly out of reach. I kick my feet with every ounce of energy to get another breath, but I swallow a mouthful of water and feel my larynx begins to constrict.

My final thoughts, as the light begins to fade, are beyond desperation. I am drowning. Nate is drowning. And there's nothing I can do to save either of us.

SERENITY RANCH

EIGHT YEARS LATER…

SERENITY RANCH

CHAPTER 1

Ellensburg is a sleepy, little college town at the junction of Interstate-90 and the Cascade Mountains. It is a rural community with approximately 8,000 residents. When the summer break ends, however, the students return to campus, the population surges to nearly 20,000.

The only other prominent fact about Ellensburg is that in 1889 the city launched a bid to become the state capital of Washington until a fire destroyed much of the downtown area. The city eventually recovered from the disaster, however, Washington voters chose Olympia as the capitol seat, sixty miles north of Seattle. As a consolation prize, state officials designated Ellensburg as the home of the first four-year college in Washington State. Formerly known as the State Normal School, Central Washington University (CWU) is primarily a liberal arts school and is most recognized for its thriving Agricultural Studies programs and the opportunity to earn a Bachelor of Science in Craft Brewing.

That said, prominent CWU alumni include John Kitna, a former NFL quarterback for the Seahawks, Bengals, Lions, and Cowboys. Additionally, U.S. Marine General James "Maddog" Mattis graduated from CWU. He served as Commander, United States Central

Command, from 2010 to 2013, and the 26th Secretary of Defense under President Donald Trump from 2017 to 2019.

For me, attending CWU was the easiest way to stick it to my father. With connections like his, I could have studied at any university I wanted to attend—Harvard, Stanford, MIT, or even Yale, my father's alma mater. But, instead, I applied to only one school—Central Washington University. (I'm pleased to say that they accepted me on my *own* merits, thank you very much.)

When I started my freshman year at CWU, I thought it was the perfect place for me. I love the Pacific Northwest—but at a distance from my father. Instead, I discovered that attending school 17 miles from where my brother died and 101 miles from where my father lives could never be far enough away.

* * * * *

An older man sits at a long table staring at an empty Styrofoam cup. Aside from the exhaustion that pulls at his eyelids, his face registers no emotion. It appears that the only thing that exists in his world is the Styrofoam cup.

I pick the chair across from him because he's precisely the type of person I want to sit across from—no one is interested in him, and he's not interested in anyone else. I've made it a habit to avoid conversations with strangers—they ask too many questions. It's better to keep my head down and avoid eye contact. Eye contact always invites unwanted and unnecessary conversation.

A few other latecomers file into the room and find chairs just as the meeting begins. It's already five minutes past seven, which means it's going to be a long night. I have business to attend to, but I don't want to stay for long. The sooner Ellensburg is in my rear-view mirror, the sooner I can banish all memories of this place—they haunt me day and night.

I study the homeless man to pass the time. But, to be honest, I have no idea if he is, in fact, homeless. He may live in a beautiful house just down the street, but I doubt it. His jacket is ragged and dirty, and the zipper is missing several teeth, just like his mouth.

The smell of stale cigarette smoke assaulted me as soon as I entered the room, and now, I'm craving a cigarette. I'd light up right here if I had one on me, but I don't. I smoked my last one after I checked into the Holiday Inn an hour ago.

Despite my best efforts to keep a low profile, the news that I'm here is making the rounds. I glance around quickly and catch several eyes looking in my direction. I hear their whispers and feel their stares. They're mostly older folks, some I recognize, others I've never seen before. It's ironic—I've never told a single person in this room my last name, yet they all know that I'm the "Coleman kid."

A man seated toward the end of the long table has tears running down his face as he speaks. His name is Timothy, and I've seen him down at the tire store. It isn't the name embroidered on his shirt as much as the voice and the hands that I remember. I talked to him once and marveled about the amount of grease under his fingernails. No amount of soap or scrubbing could wash that much grease away. Even his food must smell like motor oil.

Tim talks about how much he misses his wife and kids and how grateful he is for his friends in this room. Like the whispering, I hear the stories, but I'm not listening. I've heard them all before—many times.

I am interested, however, in the plump woman sitting next to him. I've got her pegged for a cafeteria worker, not just because she's overweight and a little bit homely, but because she forgot to take off her hairnet before leaving work. From the way she's hanging on Tim's every word, these meetings must be the highlight of her day.

The woman smiles at Tim as he finishes his monologue and says, "Thanks, Timmy." She isn't at all sad that he's single and lonely—she's got a thing for him. I'm sure of it. The thought that they'll hook up tonight enters my mind, but then I hear someone call my name.

"Jake?" It's a familiar voice, and I know what he wants before he even asks, "you got anything to share tonight?"

"No, thanks. I'm just listening."

No one speaks for the next few moments, and the entire room is quiet. Then, finally, someone in a chair behind me breaks the awful silence.

"My name is Gary…and I'm an alcoholic."

* * * * *

A dozen people stay behind chatting in small circles. They pat each other on the back like they should get a prize just for showing up. It's half-past eight, and I stay in my seat until the last lingerer leaves the room.

It's just the slender man who called my name and me. I approach him from behind as he stacks copies of the "Big Book" on a shelf in the corner closet.

Without turning, he says, "I was wonderin' when ya'd end up back in here." His voice is stern but cordial and as familiar to me as my own.

It's been two years since I saw him last, but his leathery face still looks the same. It tells a story of Central Washington's scorching summers and bitter winters—neither of which take kindly to exposed flesh.

Kris Pringle is a special kind of man—the kind who's worked his whole life with nothing to show for it but his reputation. He's a real-life cowboy and one of the last of his kind.

"Ya here by choice or court order?" He asks.

I pull out a folded piece of paper from my back pocket and hand it to him.

"Uh-huh," he says, donning a pair of reading glasses. "In trouble again, I see."

"Can you just sign it, and I'll get out of here?"

"Well, ain't we awful friendly this evening?" he says, looking at me through Coke-bottle glasses. "It says here ya've been 'court-ordered to attend a…what's this," he says, repositioning his glasses, "a prison diversion program for six consecutive months commencing on May 7th."

He looks at me with a surprised look on his face. "That's tomorrow, Jake."

"I know. That's why I'm here. I've got to check in by 9:00 AM. I also have to attend recovery meetings three times a week."

"What happens if you don't?"

"I go to prison…for a year."

"*Damn*, Jake. What'd you do this time?"

"Got busted for possession, with the intent to sell."

"You just keep digging a deeper hole, don't ya?"

I don't know what to say, so I don't say anything.

"One of these days, you're gonna hit rock bottom, just like the rest of us, and I hope that day comes sooner than later, for yer sake. Your pa know about this?"

"Yeah. He got his lawyers involved before it could hit the papers."

"Guess that's why I didn't read nothin' 'bout it. Can't have the Coleman name caught up in selling *illegal* drugs, now, can we?" He cocks his head to the side and asks, "Where're they sendin' ya anyways?"

Some ranch near Wenatchee. Supposed to be some type of working cattle ranch or something."

"Ya talking about *the* ranch?" Kris asks, his voice serious again.

"I don't know. I'd never heard of it before. I guess we work 90 hours a week and attend addiction recovery meetings in the evening. Probably be singing kumbaya around a campfire before going to bed. You know…sober *shit*."

Kris's voice is serious again. "I've heard talk about that place, Jake," he says, looking me straight in the eyes. "Heard me some bad stories about some of the folks runnin' it. Ain't the kind ya wanna get caught up with, from what I hear."

"Well, my choice was Serenity Ranch or state prison, and I'm not going back to prison!"

Kris is quiet for a moment and then asks, "This time gonna be any different, Jake?" His rebuke is subtle, but it stings, nonetheless.

"I hope so," I relent.

"How's it gonna be different?"

"I don't know," I reply, the desperateness of my situation sinking in. "I'll do whatever I gotta do. I'll work the program. I'll follow all the steps."

Kris is quiet again, and I get the feeling he's not telling me something. Finally, he looks at me with love in his eyes and asks, "Then, can I give you some advice?"

Kris Pringle has been sober for 32 years. He hasn't touched a drug or drop of alcohol since the Berlin Wall came down. It's not that the fall of Communism had anything to do with his sobriety—Kris decided he'd had enough of eating out of dumpsters and smelling like urine. So when he woke up on November 9, 1989, he decided to turn his life around.

I met Kris when I was a student at CWU and got busted for drinking underage and possession of narcotics. I was at a party somewhere near campus when a neighbor made a noise complaint because some idiot drove up to the house after midnight with his stereo blasting.

The county sheriff's office and campus police responded to the call and arrested every person there. It didn't matter if they had consumed any alcohol or used any drugs. It was a major bust for law enforcement because it was only the first week of school, serious drugs were involved, and most of us were from out-of-town.

I had to enroll in an intensive outpatient program and attend 12-step meetings three times per week. I also had to find a sponsor, and Kris took me under his wing. It wasn't my first time in rehab, but Kris helped me stay sober and complete the 4-month program.

After that, I only attended meetings after I relapsed and tried to get clean on my own. That never lasted long. Still, Kris always welcomed me and wanted to help me, even when I was unwilling to help myself.

I need Kris, and he knows it. He's the only sponsor I've ever had who can hold my feet to the fire.

"First," he says, "you've got to stay in treatment. No walkin' out, just because things get tough."

"I will," I reply. "Like I said, I don't want to go back to prison."

"Good. Second, you do a *proper* Step 4 this time. I mean 100 percent, Jake—complete honesty, no matter how hard it gets."

My eyes drop to the floor. It's another rebuke—this one less subtle.

"Third, you come and see me as soon as you get out of there. I wanna put eyes on you and make sure your head is on straight."

"I will, Kris. I promise. So, are you gonna sign my attendance sheet or not?"

"Done," Kris says as he scribbles his initials and the date on the first blank line. He hands the paper back to me and holds out his right hand. We shake, and he pulls me in for a big hug.

"Listen to me, Jake," he says. "Be careful up there. I've heard about some bad shit goin' on at that ranch,"

As he turns around and walks over to the light switch at the front of the room, he looks back at me, his face as serious as the man with the Styrofoam cup.

"Don't mess around up their Jake. Just do your time and get out of there. Otherwise," he says, as he turns out the lights, "you might be wishin' you *were* in prison.

* * * * *

I'm up the following day at six o'clock because I can't lay in bed tossing and turning a minute longer. It's been another sleepless night, and I'm tired, but I can't turn my brain off anymore. When I drink, I usually pass out or blackout. Unfortunately, alcohol damages our sleep cycles, so when I stop drinking, I suffer from insomnia. There have been many times that I've started drinking again just to start sleeping again.

The difference between passing out and blacking out is that people who pass out remember the events leading up to their loss of consciousness. They remember dinking a case of beer at the Friday night football game and stumbling home. People who blackout can't remember *shit*. In fact, CRS is a common symptom of alcohol abuse. I don't know if there is an actual disease called "can't remember shit," but I've had cases of CRS that lasted for weeks.

I turn on the TV while I get dressed just as *Good Morning America* begins a special report on my father's company:

> "*Coleman Pharmaceutical Laboratories (CPL) leads the health industry in weight management products for the 21st century. Headquartered in Seattle, Washington, CPL is the American multinational corporation that developed the first prescription weight-loss drug on the market that guarantees weight management without surgery.*"
>
> "*With a proprietary formula approved by the FDA and scientifically engineered to dissolve fat cells, a monthly injection of Metaphix can regulate fat storage in the human body to within ounces—not just pounds. The award-winning secret formula is based on an individual's blood type, desired target weight, and the dosage prescribed by a CPL-affiliated doctor. Laboratory tests demonstrate that Metaphix can assist people in achieving, and maintaining, specific body weights, regardless of age, caloric intake, level of activity, or genetic composition.*"
>
> "*Last year, Coleman Pharmaceutical Laboratories generated more than US\$47 billion in revenue, placing it in the top 3 US pharmaceutical companies, just behind Johnson and Johnson and Pfizer. In addition, the company ranked in the top 200 Fortune 500 companies. CPL market shares tripled in value last year*

when the company released its newest product, Metaphlex, a safe and effective muscle growth hormone for anyone 18 and over."

"Metaphix and Metaphlex have revolutionized modern sports. In the National Football League (NFL) alone, 21 teams partnered with CPL within six months of Metaphlex hitting the market. To no one's surprise, all 32 NFL teams signed contracts with CPL after the 12 teams using Metaphlex products increased their average players' muscle mass by 36 percent. Those twelve teams also went on to make the playoffs—something none of the other 20 teams were able to do."

"Metaphix and Metaphlex transform the human body in weeks rather than months. In addition, studies show that muscle can be chemically grown in the human body almost overnight. No other product available compares with the results that one can get from a pharmaceutically enhanced therapy session using Metaphix or Metaphlex[...]."

I turn off the TV with a click of the remote. The last thing I need is to get worked up about the success of my father's company. Besides, I have more important things to deal with today.

I need to finish packing and find some breakfast before hitting the road. I wasted too much time yesterday packing up what was left in my apartment and moving it into a storage unit. I don't expect to be back this way for at least six months, and who knows, maybe even longer.

The court ordered me to check-in at Serenity Ranch at 9:00 AM. If I don't, they have the option of denying me entry and risk losing the $75,000 my father paid upfront for six months of in-patient treatment.

Seriously? What are they going to do? Lock the door and tell me to go away? It's pocket money, and my father wouldn't blink an eye before filing a lawsuit for withholding, not only necessary but court-ordered medical treatment from his son. The ranch would be filing for bankruptcy before I got back to Ellensburg.

Under normal circumstances, the clinic would have arranged transportation to ensure I didn't make any unwanted stops and get loaded along the way. Instead, my father had a car pick me up and stop in Ellensburg to take care of a few things. When they found out who he was, they didn't argue with him.

His instructions to the young driver, who looks to be in his early thirties, are to take me to Serenity Ranch and then report back to him about his "wayward son." He doesn't talk to me. He only speaks to the driver. How's that for fatherly love and emotional support?

I'm not stupid, though. I know why he has a driver in a car with untraceable license plates pick me up and drop me off—he doesn't want any news reporters or TV cameras taking pictures of his son walking out of rehab. It would be the lead story on all the evening news syndicates. What a headline that would be, "*BILLIONAIRE'S SON IN DRUG REHAB FOR THE SIXTH TIME IN SEVEN YEARS!*" (That would be hilarious!)

I have the usual breakfast from a vending machine in the hotel's lobby—Snickers and a large coffee. I need the caffeine, but I don't feel like eating. Unless there's beer in the refrigerator, I don't usually have much of a morning appetite.

Besides, they practically force patients to eat in drug rehab. I guess it's part of the treatment for addicts. We aren't known to have the healthiest eating habits—if we eat at all. It's not surprising, though—eating isn't that high of a priority. Getting loaded—that is *always* the priority.

We drive north on Highway 97 as it climbs out of the Kittitas Valley and into the foothills of the Wenatchee Mountains. I've driven this road many times, and the memories flood my mind. I used to run out here on the weekends because there wasn't much traffic. In the winter, friends and I went snowboarding at Steven's Pass. So many good times up here in the mountains.

As the old, two-lane highway climbs over Blewett Pass, the smell of ponderosa pines and wildflowers fill the car. On most days, the Kittitas Valley smells like one big, nasty cow fart. It is only when a strong wind blows from the West or when smoke from nearby forest fires congests the valley floor that it doesn't. Today, the wind *is* coming out of the West, and the sky is solid blue.

As a student, I spent most weekends outdoors because, well, first, Ellensburg isn't even listed on some maps—there's only so much a small college town has to offer. Second, I rarely went back home—if I didn't have to see my parents, then I didn't. Third, there is a small German town just over the pass named Leavenworth. Modeled after a Bavarian alpine village, it's like attending a German beer festival every day of the year.

I prefer the scenic drive over Blewett Pass even though it's slower than heading east toward Quincy, Washington. The Gorge Amphitheater is that direction, which is a popular outdoor concert venue in the high-desert country through which the Columbia River flows. I love concerts, but I hate waking up in the backseat of a smelly van with a kinked neck and no recollection of how I got there. Oh, and I also hate rivers.

Besides, I know too many people who live out near The Gorge—some who own smelly vans, others who don't own a thing. I don't need to run into any of them right now because if I get loaded on the way to rehab, Chamberlain will have my ass.

Unfortunately, this was not my first time appearing before Judge Chamberlain on drug charges. He was lenient the first time and ordered me to attend a 16-week "intensive outpatient program" in Ellensburg. They called it "IOP," which consisted of three-hour group therapy sessions four times a week. At least in IOP, I lived in my apartment and attended university classes during the day.

The second time was a different story. Chamberlain wanted to sentence me to a year in jail for possession, with the intent to sell, but the lawyer my father sent to defend me lives in an enormous house and drives a $600,000 Ferrari. He's the best around, and he worked a plea deal for me that excluded prison time. It did, however, require me to enroll in a 6-month prison diversion program at Serenity Ranch.

JASON A. DENSLEY

*****

Growing up, it was just my parents, Nate, and me. We lived in Issaquah, WA, a small but eclectic town just east of Seattle and nestled between Lake Sammamish and Tiger Mountain. Then, when I was twelve, we moved to Bellevue, the king of Seattle suburbs. It's where Jeff Bezos, Bill Gates, and Howard Schultz live. They're just a few of the billionaires that live in Washington State, but probably the best known, or at least their companies—Amazon, Microsoft, and Starbucks—which made each of them wealthier than all but a handful of countries in the modern world

After graduating from Yale, where he met my mother, my father took a job with a small pharmaceutical company that produced prenatal vitamins. I guess he made a decent living, but he had far greater ambitions for himself.

With a degree in biochemistry, he started a new line of nutritional supplements for performance athletes. It was cutting-edge stuff, and he spent nearly all his free time running tests on the compounds he put together or running the trails up and down Tiger Mountain.

I don't remember spending much time with my father, but I remember he ran marathons and that I idolized him in my youth. We often traveled with him to big races a couple of times a year. My parents called it our "family vacations," but I didn't see him much even then.

My mother played tennis in the mornings and bridge with the ladies in the afternoon. She came from a wealthy Presbyterian family in Vancouver, British Columbia, and has never worked a day in her life.

I'm not putting her down—she's just never had a job. Even when she and my father started out, her father went out of his way to make sure she lived comfortably. Her father also made sure my father knew who kept them out of the soup kitchens while they attended college.

I think that's the reason my father works as hard as he does today. He resents the fact that his father-in-law kept them from starving while he was finishing school.

My father came from a modest Catholic family in Ann Arbor, Michigan. For the better part of their marriage, my mother's family looked down upon him.

That all changed when he started Coleman Pharmaceutical Laboratories. His science experiments in the back of the garage revolutionized modern-day nutritional therapy. Let's just say that my father *isn't* a billionaire, but Forbes Magazine predicts he will be by the end of the year.

I'd say we were a normal family, but I'm not a family therapist, so who knows. We had fun when we were together, despite my father's obsession with making money and my mother's compulsion with spending it.

I watched out for Nate growing up, not just because he was my little brother but also because he was shy and didn't make friends easily. It was tough on both of us when we moved from Issaquah to Bellevue, but Nate's transition was even more challenging.

When Nate was four or five, he was diagnosed with attention deficit hyperactivity disorder, or ADHD, which kids don't understand. As a result, Nate was always on the receiving end of jokes and much teasing. If you think kids are mean to each other in public schools, kids in private schools are merciless.

I remember when Nate came home from school one day crying. Neither of our parents was around, but our au pair, Kelly, asked him why he was crying. Some boys were picking on him because he had a speech disorder. Nate knew what he wanted to say in his head, but he had difficulty forming the words with his mouth. It was one of the early signs that led to his diagnosis.

Nate got frustrated when he stuttered or took too long between words. Pretty soon, he just stopped talking altogether. Nobody knows for sure, but I think that's why I didn't hear a scream when he fell in the river.

When Nate died, our whole family fell apart. My mother blamed my father, and my father blamed me. We argued all the time, and soon my father was going to work early in the morning and coming home after everyone else was asleep.

My mother stopped playing tennis and bridge and started drinking instead. I didn't see her much after that. She isolated herself in her room and even had the staff deliver her meals there.

I went off to college not long after that, and we don't talk to each other very much anymore. For example, one of the last times I saw my father was after my third stint in rehab. He took the day off from work to drive to Portland and pick me up. Well, his driver drove him down, but he was there waiting when I was released.

We sat in silence the entire drive back to Seattle, neither of us having anything more to say to the other. It was his way of telling me I was on my own. He wouldn't be picking me up the next time I got into trouble. It was my way of saying it was better that way and not to expect anything from me in return.

I'm glad we had that conversation. It left no doubt in either of our minds where our relationship stood. We both knew it died four years earlier in the Yakima River when Nate drowned.

CHAPTER 2

US Highway 2 traces the banks of the Wenatchee River halfway across the state of Washington. The river runs 53 miles from the banks of Lake Wenatchee to the Coulee Dam and cuts a valley deep and wide. Because of its northern latitude, sections have not seen the sun overhead since the icecaps melted and the river began to flow.

The river is important because it is a tributary to the mighty Columbia River, and Chinook salmon migrate upriver each year to spawn. In addition, the water gives life to the high-desert valley and the forested hills that rise from its banks.

Serenity Ranch sits at the end of a 12-mile dirt road on the sunny side of Highway 2. Chelan County wanted to pave part of it years ago, but the owners of the 12,200-acre ranch wouldn't allow it. As a result, there are no paved roads on the 19-square miles north of Highway 2.

The land belongs to Jim and Susan Hartwell, two of the last cattle ranchers in Washington State. It is as pristine as when the Wenatchee Indians hunted bison on its rolling hills and trapped salmon in the river they named and claimed.

There are no signs directing travelers to Serenity Ranch. The dirt road that intersects Highway 2 is unmarked and easy to miss. The ranch is challenging to find even with GPS because very few maps place labels on private property.

The 10-foot chain-link fence surrounding the property is set back three miles from Highway 2 and monitored by security cameras. In addition, the gate which deters curious visitors is nearly always locked. No one gets in without permission, and no one leaves unless permitted. While the "no trespassing" signs, video cameras, and chain-link fences are strong deterrents, it's the three-foot section of razor-sharp concertina wire sitting atop the fence that sends the most ardent warning. As a result, very few visitors drop by unannounced.

The rolled concertina wire looks out of place to the casual observer, especially among the tall spruce and basalt spires that are part of the natural habitat. It could also be seen as overkill if its only intended purpose was to contain the lazy cattle grazing in the grassy meadows within.

Some people justifiably question whether the fence keeps the uninvited out or the inhabitants within. Either way, one must assume that more goes on in the fenced enclosure than raising beef cattle destined for slaughterhouses.

*****

The Mercedes Benz S580 grinds to a halt in the gravel parking lot next to a solitary cabin. A sign, hand-carved by Dr. Hartman himself, hangs above the front door and reads, "Find Peace at Serenity Ranch."

A brand-new Ford F-350 Crew Cab pick-up truck is parked next to the building. The initials SR, inside a diamond, are stenciled on the front doors and the extended wheel wells above the dual rear tires.

My driver turns off the car and opens his door before the dirt settles back on the road. But, unfortunately, he realizes his mistake seconds too late. He lets out an audible sigh as fine dust particles fill the interior of the vehicle. (I can't wait until he sees what's happened to his immaculately polished paint job.) It's now impossible to distinguish the color of the car or see through the windows. The windshield is the only window that offers visibility, and only then because he used the wiper blades to help him stay on the road.

I grab my cell phone and earbuds from the back seat and stuff them in the small backpack I brought with me. I packed one other bag with a few pairs of jeans, t-shirts, socks, underwear, and toiletries. There were no instructions about what to bring, so I packed light. I figure I can beg, borrow, or steal any other items I need.

From my experiences, these rehab facilities are pretty much all the same—lots of group therapy sessions, medication, meditation, and maybe some acupuncture, or a massage, once a week. Their purpose is to heal the mind, body, and soul.

The driver pulls my bag from the trunk and sets it on the stairs leading up to the cabin. He's in a hurry to get back to the big city. One night away from Seattle, and he's going through Starbucks withdrawal.

The front door opens just as I start up the stairs. A gorgeous woman, dressed in a western shirt and faded blue jeans, stands in the doorway. "Well, you must be Jacob."

"It's Jake," I reply, as the scent of her perfume catches me off-guard.

The white button-down shirt is tight on her bosom, and the tailored jeans accentuate the long, slender legs that give them shape. Her hair is long and black, and her eyes are hungry.

Her eyes undress me several times as I climb the steps and stop on the stair just below her. I can't go any further because she blocks the doorway. I can tell she enjoys controlling our encounter because she makes no effort to let me pass.

"Is this where I check in?"

After a distinct pause, she turns sideways in the doorway and says, "Please, come inside." I don't know if she intends to or not, but she brushes against me with her chest as I sidestep through the doorway with a bag in each hand.

Looking back at the car, she says, "I had one like that not too long ago."

"An S-series Mercedes?"

"No. The sexy driver in the black tailored suit."

* * * * *

I'm too stunned to do anything for the next few seconds, so I just stand there until I hear someone shuffling papers to my right. Then, turning, I see an older woman sitting at a desk. For some strange reason, I didn't even notice her when I walked in.

"Have a seat," she says impatiently, motioning to the chair I'm standing by. "Hard time finding us?"

"Not really," I reply, trying to remember the drive from Ellensburg. "The driver went slow because he didn't want to kick up any rocks and scratch the side of the car."

I peer out the windows at the rugged mountains in the distance. "I had no idea this place was up here."

"We try to keep to ourselves as much as possible," she says. My name is Susan, but people call me 'Sue.' You want something to drink?"

"Is a Whiskey Sour out of the question?"

"I'll get you a water," she says, with an edginess to her voice. "There are some forms I need you to fill out before I hand you over to our medical staff."

"Was that one of the nurses I just met?"

"Hardly!" Sue replies, looking at me sharply. "That's Dr. Hartwell's oldest daughter, Vanessa. You best stay far away from her."

"Who's Dr. Hartwell?"

"He's the director here at Serenity Ranch, and he's very protective of his flock," she says, handing me a clipboard with several forms and a pen. "He doesn't take kindly to wolves getting in the barn."

"Maybe someone should tell *her* that," I reply, wondering why I'm the one mistaken as the predator.

Sue gives me a stern look as she leaves the room and returns moments later with a bottle of water. She's a serious woman with no discernable sense of humor whatsoever.

I sigh as I sit back in the chair and thumb through the pages. It's the same as all other intakes I've been through in the past—medical history, drug or alcohol abuse questionnaire, emergency contact information, release forms, billing information, and so on.

I want to ask why they didn't forward my records from the treatment center I just left, but Sue doesn't strike me as someone who likes to answer questions. It would save a tree if they had, though—not that I'm an environmentalist or anything. I just have a long history of drug *and* alcohol abuse.

I don't bother to read all the small print as I fill out the paperwork. I am well aware that federal laws exist to protect my privacy and that state law requires the reporting of suspected child abuse and neglect. However, when I see that disclaimer, I wonder if parents who are so emotionally f--ked-up that they want nothing to do with their kids are ever charged with neglect?

The standard paperwork also includes the usual warnings. For example, patients cannot bring drugs or alcohol into rehab facilities, even if prescribed by a doctor. (Wow! Who'd have thought!?) Even then, a doctor must review the required medications to ensure the safety of the patient and the staff.

There is even a list of prohibited items that include guns, knives, scissors, disposable razors, nail clippers, belts, and shoelaces—basically, anything someone might use to hurt themselves or others. (Seriously? Do they really think I'm going to slice my wrists with a pair of nail clippers?)

Furthermore, I am free to walk out of the facility at any time unless I have been sent here by legal court order and do not complete treatment. In that case, I will be arrested by local authorities and returned to the court that has jurisdiction over me.

Blah, Blah, Blah. It still takes me almost an hour to fill out all the paperwork. When I finish, I hand the clipboard back to Sue, and she picks up the phone and dials a number.

"Come and get him," she says and hangs up the phone. Moments later, a male nurse walks in wearing hospital scrubs.

"Follow me," he says and takes me into a small room with a couple of chairs and a long table. "Let's start with your vitals, and then we'll go over your medical history."

"Okay," I say, sitting on the edge of the table, kicking my feet. The nurse takes my pulse, blood pressure, and temperature and writes them on my chart.

"You a runner?" he asks.

"Yeah. I used to run marathons, but I haven't been running much the last couple of years."

"Your heart rate and blood pressure are low," he explains. "Most people that come in here have high blood pressure and a fast heart rate—typical withdrawal symptoms. But, I noticed that your hands aren't shaking, and your eyes look normal. When did you use last?"

"Over a month ago. I just got released from an in-patient facility in Tacoma."

"I see," he nods, "so you've already been through detox. This place is the first stop for most people that come through here, and they're usually in bad shape for the first week or so. At least you won't be seeing any pink elephants, right?"

I understand the joke, but I don't find it funny. I had "the DTs," or delirium tremens, once, and I thought I was going to die.

Seeing pink elephants refer to withdrawal delirium—a severe form of alcohol withdrawal that usually appears after long periods of heavy drinking. Medical books characterize it as "the rapid onset of severe confusion, uncontrollable tremors, and hallucinations."[1]

The term originates from an alcoholic character in Jack London's 1913 novel *John Barleycorn*, who hallucinates pink elephants. Years

---

[1] https://en.wikipedia.org/wiki/Delirium_Tremens

later, the main character in the Disney film "Dumbo" unintentionally gets drunk and sees an entire parade of pink elephants.

Part of recovering from drugs and alcohol is learning what drugs (and alcohol is a drug) do to the brain. For example, a part of our brain is called the "reward center," and drugs work on that reward center by causing the body to release significant quantities of a chemical called dopamine. Dopamine is a neurotransmitter in our brains that give us pleasurable feelings, like when drinking a cup of coffee in the morning or having sex.

Repeated use of drugs and alcohol changes the neuropathways in our brains. For one thing, our brains begin to produce less of the chemical and reduce the number of dopamine receptors. That means that our tolerance level increases, and we need larger amounts of drugs and alcohol to get the same "high."

Another result of repeated drug and alcohol use is that the body becomes dependent on it over time. This chemical dependence is known as addiction, and when addicts suddenly stop using, they experience withdrawal symptoms.

Most drugs have some withdrawal symptoms associated with them, but some are more dangerous than others. I've tried to quit drinking on my own several times. Unfortunately, while I haven't seen any pink elephants, I have experienced my share of withdrawal symptoms—and they can be excruciating.

At a *minimum*, after a long period of drinking, my hands shake so badly that I can't write my name. At their worst, I've had severe seizures and ended up in the hospital. I guess I've been fortunate, though; others die from it.

It's true. People say that alcohol and drugs kill people, but after becoming chemically dependent, a person can die from the shock of stopping all at once. A strange as it sounds, many doctors say it is better to wean heavy drinkers off alcohol than cut them off "cold turkey."

I know a guy who tried to stop drinking and got the DTs so bad that he began hallucinating and having seizures just 12 hours after his last drink. When his girlfriend called 9-1-1, and the ambulance showed up, the paramedics asked if there was any alcohol in the house. When she told them there was some beer in the refrigerator, one medic grabbed a beer and made my buddy drink it. The medic took another in the ambulance just in case he had another seizure on the way to the hospital. (I think that dude may have coined the phrase "one more for the road.")

"Okay, roll up your sleeves," the nurse says. "I've got to draw some blood."

"With nail clippers?" I ask as I push up my sleeves above my elbows.

"What?"

"Never mind. Which arm do you want?"

"Doesn't matter." He gets an intravenous needle and an empty vial ready, but when he sees my arms, his eyes get big. "O-M-G!"

It can be difficult for someone who never uses drugs to imagine why someone would use a needle to inject drugs. But, for people like me, it's a no-brainer.

When you swallow a pill, it takes somewhere between 15 minutes and 1 hour to fully dissolve in your blood, So one way to speed things up is to crush and snort the pill. After a while, though, you begin to build your tolerance and need higher quantities, or more potent drugs, to get the same high.

After snorting drugs for a while, many users turn to shooting up because the effects are nearly instantaneous, and it's a more intense high because you get the full impact right away. It is more painful and dangerous—with people swapping needles and overdosing—but to the addict, it's worth it.

There's no way to explain what it's like shooting up with heroin or fentanyl. It's a high like no other and more pleasurable than anything I've ever imagined. It's why they are so addictive. The problem is that the high doesn't last very long. And, they say, "there's no high like the first high," so you shoot up again and again—until you get help or end up dead.

It's easy to spot track marks in someone's arms. Older track marks turn into light pink or white scars. If the vein gets damaged from shooting up, it gets darker and more noticeable under the skin.

When you've used drugs as long as I have, it's hard to hide track marks. Hence, some people start shooting up in their feet, between their toes, legs, and groin areas to keep others from noticing. (So, if you ever wonder if someone is shooting drugs intravenously, and they're wearing long sleeves in the middle of summer, you already know.)

When you get to the point that you don't care anymore, your arms start to look like mine. I've got scars all over my wrists and forearms. I have permanent bruises under my skin, and my arms look as if they've been severely burned in places.

The nurse looks at my arms and can't find a good vein, so he goes for one on the back of my hand.

"You'll never get that one," I tell him as he wipes the area with an alcohol pad.

He sticks me in a vein just below my middle knuckle, but it rolls to the side, and the needle doesn't penetrate. I knew it wouldn't—it's like trying to get a wet worm on a hook—that one's shot (no pun intended).

"Here, let me do it," I say, grabbing the butterfly needle and sticking it in a vein just above my wrist. "That one's hard to see, but it's my 'go-to' when all others fail me."

The nurse fills four vials of blood, hands me the gauze strip, and lets me pull the needle out of my arm. He reaches for a band-aid, but I pull my sleeves back down, and he leaves me alone.

"I need to go over your history with drugs and alcohol."

"Why didn't they send my records over from Tacoma?" I ask. "I just went through this with them a month ago. It *hasn't* changed."

His answer shouldn't surprise me, but it does. "I asked the same question," he replies. "A King County judge issued a court order the day you entered treatment which prohibits any disclosure of your records, even between medical facilities or medical staff."

"Great! Thanks, Dad," I say a bit too loud.

"What's that?"

"Nothing. I'll answer the questions again."

He goes back to the forms I filled out earlier. "Let's see. You indicated that you used alcohol, nicotine, heroin, cocaine, and opioids within the last six months. Is that correct?"

"Yup."

"What opioids do you use?"

"Kickers, percs, 357s, gum…."

"Hold on a second," he says, trying to write the formal drug names. "Oxycodone, Percocet, Hydrocodone, opium. Any others?"

I shrug my shoulders. "Nah…that's about it."

"What about benzodiazepines?"

"Benzos? Yeah, but not in the last six months."

"How long ago did you use them?"

"Oh man, I quit those a couple of years ago. Couldn't stand the nightmares."

"Any other drugs we haven't mentioned?"

"Just ecstasy."

"When did you last use ecstasy?"

"I don't know the date. It was the night I tried to kill myself."

"Tell me about that?"

"No," I reply, cursing myself for even mentioning it. "I don't talk about that."

"Did something happen?"

"I told you, I don't talk about it."

"Okay…but understanding what triggers you might help us avoid a situation where you feel like hurting yourself again—or others."

I'm trying hard to keep my cool, but I'm starting to get very upset. "Seriously, man. I don't want to talk about it. If you ask me again, I'm going to punch you in the throat!"

"Whoa," he says, "take it easy. I didn't mean to upset you. Let's move on to something else. You said you've been in treatment four times before this."

"Yup." I go from angry to bored just as quickly as I get upset. It's just the way I am. I can be laughing one minute and crying the next.

"You were admitted to Inner Peace in Tacoma about six years ago and completed all 30 days of in-patient therapy. Is that right?"

"Yes."

After that, you did four months of *outpatient* therapy at Northwest Recovery in Ellensburg. How long were you clean after that?"

"I think I got seven months," I say, trying to remember the longest period of sobriety I've had in eight years.

"What was your 'drug of choice' back then?"

"My 'D-O-C?' Alcohol. Our house was full of it. My father always had dinner parties, and my mother started drinking in the afternoon. Alcohol was easy to get."

"After your relapse...?"

I *hate* that word—relapse! Therapists always say, "relapse is just a part of recovery." They make it sound like it's okay. That's *bullshit!* That's like telling someone who keeps getting in fender benders they just need another accident to become a better driver.

"...you were admitted to The Recovery Center in Seattle. You stayed eleven days and then checked yourself out. Did you start using right away?"

"Yeah. By that time, I was smoking weed and snorting Oxy when I could get it."

"How did you get access to OxyContin?"

"My mother always had some around. She broke her collar bone, playing tennis, I think. She said it never healed right—she was always in pain. She should be in rehab, not me."

"Okay," he says, "After that, you were arrested for possession of a controlled substance and entered treatment at New Life? That's in California, right? I think I've seen their TV commercials. Looks nice!"

"Yeah, it's in Malibu, but it's a joke. It's a place for Hollywood stars and rich kids. Celebrities go there to detox for a week, and they come out magically cured."

"I met one famous guy—I'd tell you his name, but I'm sure I'd get sued—anyway, he was there for his *eleventh* time. That place is just a luxury retreat—people don't find sobriety there."

"When did you start using heroin?"

"When I started college and found others who like to party. Man, my grades were *atrocious* that first year! That was about the time my father said he wasn't going to support me anymore if I didn't get clean."

"When I walked out of New Life, he cut me off completely—no allowance, no college, nothing. I had some money in the bank, so I was okay at first, but I had my own place, and I was shooting up every day. That went on for over a year. Eventually, the money ran out."

"And then you ended up back in Tacoma?" He asks, carefully sidestepping the incident that landed me in the hospital and then jail.

"Yup."

I know he wants to ask more questions, but he wisely moves on.

"Okay. Just one more question. What are your feelings about religion, or, as some prefer to call it— the spiritual side of recovery?"

"It doesn't work for me."

"Was your family religious?"

"I was baptized into the Catholic church when I was a baby and went to church with my family. We didn't go a lot, but you know, we attended mass on Easter and Christmas Eve."

"When I was about sixteen, my brother Nate died in an accident, and we just stopped going. We pretty much stopped doing anything together at that point. My father was always at work, and my mother, well, I've already told you about her."

"So, you don't consider yourself 'spiritual' any longer?"

My answer is final. "I'm not into the '*God thing*,' okay?"

"Okay, that's all the questions I have. I just need to look at your things," he says, pointing to my bags on the floor.

This part of the process always pisses me off. I don't like people going through my stuff. Never have.

When I bend down to pick them up, he says, "I got it. You're not allowed to touch your bags during this part of the screening.

"I'm not allowed to touch my *own* bags?"

"Sorry, it's the rules. I have to search for any prohibited items that you can't bring into the facility. You can watch, but you can't touch anything while I go through them."

"Whatever." I'm tired of this dude already.

One by one, the nurse goes through every pocket, compartment, zipper, strap, nook, crevice, and cranny, looking for prohibited items. When he stops, my things are scattered all over the table; every single item of clothing, toiletries, and all my personal items are on display.

"Okay, take everything out of your pockets," he says.

I don't hide the irritation in my voice any longer. "If you're going to strip search me, I hope you tip well because I don't do this for free."

He ignores me and waits for me to empty my pockets. The only contraband he finds is my cell phone, my shoelaces, and a belt I had in my luggage.

"I need your phone, belt, and shoelaces."

They always take your phone in these places. They think you're going to make a call and have someone drop a duffel bag full of crystal meth from a drone. (I guess I shouldn't be so cynical—no doubt someone's tried it.)

Of course, they always take your belt too. (I know, I should have known better.) Tons of addicts have hung themselves rather than try to live without drugs. For some people, it just isn't possible to get clean.

Never, however, has anyone ever taken my shoelaces.

"What if my shoes fall off?"

"Not my problem."

"Do you think I'm going to hang myself with a pair of Converse All-Stars?

"Those are the rules. You may not like them, but, like I said—it's not my problem."

It's not even worth arguing anymore. I pull the laces out of my shoes and hand them to him. In return, he gives me two jumbo heavy-duty rubber bands, the kind you'd put around a crocodile's mouth to keep it from eating you.

"What are these for?"

"To keep your shoes on until you get your boots."

"*Boots*?"

"You don't have any boots?" he asks. "This is a ranch. You can't go around in a pair of Converse high tops."

"Watch me," I say.

I pack everything back up and toss the bag on the floor. Now one of my shirts is stuck in the zipper. I'm just about to go off on this dude. All I want to do is get to my room. It'd better be a private room with a TV and a mini-fridge. Besides, I've done more talking today than I usually do in a month.

"I've got a few more questions I need you to answer before we go on."

"Oh my *God*! What else could you possibly want to know about me that I haven't told you already?"

"Relax. They just need to find out where you'll fit in the best here at the ranch. The foreman usually asks these questions, but he's out pulling a calf."

While he shuffles between pages, I ask, "Why's he pulling a calf? Is he running or something?"

"A *calf*, dumbass. You know? A baby cow?"

"Oh, right."

"Here it is. Work qualifications. First question. Can you ride a horse?"

"Of course," I lie. (I've never been anywhere near a horse.)

"Can you walk more than one horse at a time?"

"Uh, probably," I say, with less confidence than my last answer.

"Do you have any experience driving tractors or 18-wheelers?

"What?"

"I'll take that as a 'no,'" he says, writing something on the clipboard. "Can you lift 80 pounds?"

"80 pounds of what?"

"Doesn't matter. Can you lift 80 pounds?"

"I guess so."

"Any experience with calving, branding, or castration?"

"What the…?" I put my hands to my mouth, realizing I have no idea what I've gotten myself into.

"Ever worked in a slaughterhouse?"

"No!"

He marks the appropriate block and continues. "Do you have any experience with welding, electrical, or chainsaw operations?"

"Okay. Hold on! You take my shoelaces but ask if I can use a chainsaw? What kind of twisted place *is* this?"

"When was your last tetanus shot?"

"No idea," I reply as I begin to realize the horrors that await me.

"Well, we'll take care of that right now." He pulls a syringe from a pocket in his scrubs and breaks off the protective cap over the needle. "I think this one is Tetanus," he says. "Or is this the deworming one?"

Before I can even blink, he wipes my shoulder with an alcohol swab and jabs me with the needle.

"Ouch!" I yell, jumping out of my chair as soon as he withdraws the needle.

"Okay," he says, "I think we're all done here. Ready to see the ranch?"

I'm still rubbing my arm a few minutes later as I sit in the passenger seat next to Sue. She's talking to someone named 'Pit Bull' on a 2-meter radio. It sounds like there's a problem with the new calf, and Sue isn't happy. (I get the feeling Sue is *never* happy.)

We take another dirt road further up the mountain from the reception building, and I start to realize just how big this ranch is. We drive 20 minutes, and there is nothing but green pastures, rolling hills, and several herds of cattle grazing in the fields.

As we drive over a slight rise, a spacious valley comes into view, its bottom covered by a pristine lake. The water is so clear I can see the pilings extending several yards underwater at the base of an expansive pier. The backdrop is monolithic walls of basalt rock rising hundreds of meters above the valley floor.

Six cozy cabins sit on the hillside above the lake. Each cabin has a small deck with wooden chairs and a set of stairs leading up to the front door. Firewood is stacked in the corner on each deck, awaiting colder months when the lake freezes over and deep snow covers the ground.

A majestic lodge stands on the crown of the hill overlooking the valley. The building is stately and made of wood and stone, which came from the surrounding hills. It reminds me of a grand ski lodge I once saw in British Columbia, Canada. A large corral with a dozen horses sits a bit further back, their coats gleaming in the afternoon sun.

I'm not easily impressed with big houses or sprawling estates, but the grandeur of this site is indescribable. With the afternoon sun perched atop a cloudless sky and the entire landscape mirrored on the surface of the lake, it is, without a doubt, the most spectacular view I have ever seen.

It's obvious now why they call this place Serenity Ranch.

CHAPTER 3

"This is where you'll bunk," Sue says as she parks the truck near one of the cabins and gets out. I get my bags out of the truck bed and give them a good kick, trying unsuccessfully to remove the thick layer of dust that covers them both.

When we walk in, I notice the curtains in the cabin are closed, and the only light coming in is through the door. Still, it isn't hard to see the dimensions of the one-room cabin with its wood floor and open ceiling up to the timbers on the roof.

Sue turns on the lights, and I see two sets of bunk beds on opposite walls, a pair of four-drawer dressers on another, and a wood-burning stove near the front door. There's only one other door in the room, and I'm hoping there's a toilet and a shower in there.

I have to admit my surprise. The beds are made, the pillows fluffed, and the sheets folded with hospital corners. One of the dresser drawers is partially open, and I can see that someone meticulously folded the shirts inside. There isn't an article of clothing, piece of garbage, or a single crumb on the floor. It's hard to believe anyone lives here at all. I'm betting this place has maid service.

Sue, however, has a different impression. She pulls a couple of other drawers open and looks inside. After that, she walks over to one of the beds and pinches the wool blanket in the middle to see if it is taut. Finally, she opens the bathroom door, looks inside, and shuts it again. I don't know what she was expecting, but I can tell she doesn't like what she sees.

"Top bunk's yours," she says. "'Terd' has the bottom."

"Terd?" I ask.

"It's 'Todd,' everyone calls him 'Terd.'"

"Nice," I say under my breath. "Where's everybody now?"

"They're at the chow hall. I'll take you there after you get changed."

Walking back to the front door, she stops and looks back at me, standing in the middle of the room. I'm wearing a wrinkled t-shirt, a pair of basketball shorts, and high-top sneakers. I know she thinks I'm an idiot.

"'Round here, we wear long pants and boots. The rattlesnakes ain't friendly in these parts, and the mosquitos are as big as birds. Get changed. I'll be waitin' for you outside."

I change out of the shorts I'm wearing and throw on a pair of jeans. The shoes with the rubber bands will have to do until I can find something better.

I look around the cabin, and reality begins to set in for me. There won't be any late-night TV because there isn't one. I just pray there's a place to charge my iPod.

When I walk out the front door, Sue is on the radio again and madder than hell. I hear, "...if this place ain't cleaned up by first light, they bunk in the barn until it is."

A crisp "copy" comes over the radio, "be down for supper after I get this calf fed. It's a shame her mama bled out. I really thought she was gonna make it."

I've heard that sailors curse a lot, but I don't think anyone could hold a candle to Sue. I've been around some salty characters in my life, but I've never heard anyone cuss like her.

I feel like I'm back in a high school locker room. In one sentence, Sue curses eleven times, and that's only the one about a priest, a mule, and a meat cleaver. I'm no saint, but I could never repeat what she just said. Unfortunately, I have a mental picture of what she described, and I will never get that out of my head.

"So, here's the deal," Sue says after she calms down and we start up the hill toward a pre-fabricated building made of metal sheeting. "5:00 AM wake up. Morning chores start at 5:30. You'll be milkin' cows, muckin' corrals, feedin' cows, or gatherin' eggs. Your bunkmates will show you what to do. Jobs rotate weekly between the four cabins."

"Wait," I say, not sure if I heard her right. "Did you just say 5:00 AM *wake up*?"

"Jake, this is a cattle ranch, and cows wake up early—we ain't got time to mess around. Breakfast is at 7:00. You'll get your work assignments at the horse corrals at 7:30. Lunch is back here at noon; unless you're movin' cattle, then you'll be packin' your lunch and eatin' on the trail. Back here at 5:00 for dinner, then evenin' chores at 6:00. Them support group meetings y'all do are from 7:00 to 8:00 every other night, but the rest of the time is yours. Oh, and it's lights out at 9:00 PM."

Sue pushes the front door open, and I follow her inside. What looks like a large shed is actually a cafeteria where meals are prepared in a back kitchen and served upfront by ladies in hairnets. I know what it is now because a sign over the door says, "Chow Hall". The funny thing is, the sign is on the inside.

There are six tables with five to six people seated at each. Most look my age, but a few are older, maybe in their thirties or forties. The older crowd is sitting at a table of their own. They look to me like they're real cowboys, with hats, boots, and buckles. The rest are a rag-tag bunch of wannabes who look nothing like cowboys. I know because they all look like me—skinny, street punks who don't know the first thing about ranching.

"Listen up," Sue yells. The room goes silent, and all eyes turn toward us. She acknowledges the cowboys in the room, "Sorry to disturb your supper gents, but I need to have a word with these jacklegs."

"A few years ago, this was the top producing beef ranch in the state. We had cows from here to the Columbia River. My family earned their reputation by the sweat of their brow. They worked hard to build a cattle empire."

"I inherited this ranch and have worked it my entire life.

"Eight years ago," she says, wiping a tear, "Dr. Hartwell had a vision and saw a truly divine purpose for this land. This ain't just a working cattle ranch anymore—it's a place where addicts and alcoholics can learn to make something of themselves and begin a new life."

"We have taken y'all in to help you to change your lives. All we ask is that you work hard and take care of this place. Keep it clean. Keep it tidy. Take a little pride in the things you're part of."

"But a few minutes ago, I saw a cabin that was *not* clean. It was *not* tidy. It was *not* acceptable. Because of that, it's lights out at 8:00 P.M. tonight. Y'all just lost an hour of personal time tonight, and your cabins better be spotless when I come around after breakfast. One thing you're gonna learn around here is that everyone does their part. I ain't your momma, and I ain't cleanin' up after you. I've got a beef ranch to run. Is that understood?"

I expect to hear groans and complaints, but everyone in the room, including me says, "Yes, ma'am."

Finally, Sue looks at me and says, "This is Jake. He's bunkin' with Cabin 2. Drew, Seth, Terd—you guys show him the ropes. I'll be around to lock up after your meeting."

* * * * *

As soon as Sue finishes her speech and walks out, the room empties, and I'm left standing alone in the chow hall.

I'm not hungry, but I don't know what to do, so I walk through the line with a tray and pick up a bag of potato chips and a gingerbread cookie.

"Uh, I don't think so, mister."

Behind me stands a big black woman in a white apron with her hands on her hips. She has a look of disappointment on her face. I turn around to see her dishing up a bowl of chili and putting it on a plate next to a large piece of cornbread.

"You like cheese?" She asks as she picks up a handful of shredded cheddar cheese and sprinkles it on the chili. She tops it off with sliced jalapenos and sour cream—none of it sounding even the slightest bit appetizing.

"How 'bout some slaw?" Before I realize what she's doing, she's fixed me a whole plate of food and set it down at the table in front of me.

"Now let's get one thing straight," she says, her hands back on her hips, "you gonna *eat* 'round here."

I sit down because I don't know what she'll do if I don't.

"Thanks, but I'm not all that hungry."

"Bein' hungry ain't got nothin' to do with it, son. You gonna be workin' round here, and that means you got to eat. Never know when you might ride out in a storm and get stuck out there for two, maybe three days. So 'round here, eatin' is as important as breathin'."

"Okay," I say as I get ready to take my first bite.

"Hold on, son," she says with a surprised look. "You don't say grace before ya eat?"

"No," I confess.

"Well, we gonna say grace first," she says, taking both my hands in hers and closing her eyes. "Lord, thank you for this food and the hands that prepared it. Bless it that we have the strength to do thy work, and bless Jake, here, that he gets along good with the other boys. In Jesus' name, amen."

At this point, I feel like I'm going into shock. Maybe it's holding hands with someone I just met, but it feels like I'm having an out-of-body experience. The only reason I know I'm not is because, after my first spoonful of chili, my tastebuds are melting, and my mouth is on broil.

"I got to get back to the kitchen, but you sit here and finish your supper. Them other boys will be in the cabins waitin' on ya, but they ain't goin' nowhere. Sue likes an orderly place. Keeps people disciplined, she says."

When I finish, I clear my tray and yell, "thank you." But, unfortunately, I'm not sure anyone hears me.

A shiver runs down my back as I walk out into the night and light a cigarette. I don't know what's worse, realizing I have no idea what the next six months have in store for me or that I have no place to go when I leave. It's the most alone I've ever felt—except for every other moment since Nate died.

* * * * *

I'm in no hurry to get to the cabin as my mind is still processing all that has happened since I arrived. The shades still cover the windows, but I understand why. For the occupants, it's their last bastion of privacy in a world where self-isolation and hidden secrets are a thing of the past.

In recovery circles, they say that "you are only as sick as your secrets." I guess that's true. A secret kept in the dark grows and becomes more harmful. Once it's out in the open, it loses its power. Recovery has a way of revealing the truth about everything and everyone.

I try to peak through the crack between the shades and window frame, but I can only see into an empty corner. I do hear voices, however, and none of them sound happy.

As I push the front door open, a shoe comes flying across the room and hits the wall next to my head. I see one guy on the ground, his lower lip bleeding, and a tall kid holding back another who wants back at the guy on the floor. They ignore me as if I'm not standing there.

"I told you not to touch my shit!" The angry kid says as he wrestles to get out of the other guy's arms.

The one on the floor rubs his mouth, "I just wanted to look at it, Seth. What's your problem?"

"Chill out, Seth," the tallest boy says, still holding the other back. "You're gonna get us all in trouble. You heard what Sue said—we gotta clean up this place."

"I ain't scared of Sue," Seth argues and shrugs off the taller boy's hold.

The boy with the bloody lip picks up a small photograph from the floor and hands it to Seth. "I just wanted to look at it for a second. She's pretty. I wasn't tryin' to make you mad.

Seth takes the picture and sticks it between two pages in a book on his bed. "Just don't be goin' 'round touchin' things that ain't yours, okay?

I'm still standing in the open doorway when the tall kid notices me. "Hey, man, c'mon in. Don't mind us, just a little family drama, you know?"

"Yeah, no, it's okay. I didn't mean to walk in on you all like that."

The tall kid walks over and extends his hand—very formal-like. He introduces himself as Drew, the other guy as Seth, and the dude with the fat lip as Terd.

"Jake," I reply, "guess I'm the fourth horseman."

Terd hurries over and does the same. "It's Todd, but everyone calls me Terd."

"Why's that?" I ask.

"You don't wanna know," Drew says as he falls onto his bunk across the room.

"Yeah," Seth says, "you'll find out in an hour or so. But, I don't recommend following him into the bathroom. He clogs the toilet at least once a day. Sue even got him his own plunger and wrote his name on it, didn't she, Terd?"

Todd ignores Seth, but I can tell he's embarrassed.

"Which drawers are mine?"

Todd walks over to one of the dressers and pulls open the bottom two drawers. "These two are yours," he says, pulling a pair of underwear out of one of the drawers. "Huh, I was wondering where these went."

"Okay. Thanks. And I guess I'm in that top bunk?"

"Unless you want the bottom," Terd says, "which is fine with me. I can switch with you if you want. Heights don't bother me at all. In fact, I went bungee jumping on acid one time. I totally thought I was going to smash into the ground. Have you ever done that?"

"No, but I'm good with the top bunk," I say, realizing that if I don't cut him off, I could learn everything about Terd in a single night.

Terd opens the top drawer to return his lost underwear, so I ask about the contents.

"You fold your underwear, Todd?"

"Yeah, we all do. It's part of the program," he replies. "Check it out." He opens his other drawer to show me a stack of carefully folded t-shirts, each one a six-inch square. We get inspected once in a while. Sue is a 'neat-freak' and says 'a clean room is the sign of a clear mind.'"

"I think it's the sign of a *sick* mind," Seth declares. "Where you from, Jake?"

"Issaquah," I lie. Over the past several years, I've learned that it isn't a good idea to tell a bunch of addicts that your family lives next door to Bill Gates. I've had several acquaintances come right up to the security gate in our neighborhood asking for money. I can assure you that my father was not happy.

"Where's that?" Drew asks, "never heard of it."

"It's 17 miles southeast of Seattle on Interstate-90," Terd says before I can form a response.

"Shut up, Terd," Seth says, laying on his bunk with his eyes closed. "You're such a nerd. That's a good one—Terd the Nerd."

"Seattle, huh? You know Bill Gates?" Drew asks jokingly.

"Nah," I lie again. "I live in Ellensburg now and don't get back home too often. Where you guys from?"

"I'm from Utah—Salt Lake City," Drew answers, "Seth's from Spokane and Terd's from Portland."

"How'd you guys end up here?" I ask, trying to keep the focus on anyone else but myself.

"I *wanted* to come here," Drew says excitedly. "This place is *awesome*! I love the mountains and being outdoors. My uncle has a ranch in Cedar City, Utah, and I'm gonna go work for him after this."

"You here for drugs and alcohol, though, right?" I ask, surprised that anyone would voluntarily go to rehab because they like being outside.

Seth immediately opens his eyes and sits up in his bunk. "Check this out," he says, laughing, "Drew read about this place on a blog, right? So, he goes out and buys some NoDoz at the grocery store, crushes them up, sticks 'em in a baggie, and hides 'em in his underwear drawer. His mom finds 'em when she does the laundry and tells his dad. When they confront him about it, he tells them it's cocaine."

Seth is laughing so hard he can hardly finish the story.

"He tells them he knows he's got a problem and has been looking into this rehab center up in Washington State. So they fork out the money and send him here."

"You lied to get into rehab?" I ask.

"Yeah," Drew says as he gives Seth 'the bird. "But that's not all true. The insurance paid for most of it—my parents just had to pay the deductible."

Seth, Todd, and I are all laughing now.

"Shut up, Seth." Drew counters, "at least I don't go around abusing animals. You're the one who set the neighbor's dog on fire!"

"No, I didn't," Seth argues. "I lit a bottle rocket and shot it into my neighbor's garage. How was I supposed to know the dog was in there."

"What about you?" Drew asks, "What're you in here for?"

"Drugs and alcohol," I say, "mostly drugs."

"What's your D-O-C?"

For the second time today, I tell my new bunkmates how I ended up getting busted for possession with the intent to sell. They seem satisfied with just the latter part of the story, which saves me from spilling my entire medical history once again.

It turns out that Drew's been here the longest at almost three months, Seth two months, and Terd five weeks. They seem like okay guys, but I'd still rather have a private room.

I unpack my bags and climb up on my bunk to find out more about this place. "So, what's Sue's deal?" I ask, "She always pissed off like that?"

"Pretty much. The Warden ain't doin' too well these days. She's got a lot of pressure on her runnin' things around her," Drew says.

"Wait, who's the Warden?

"Sue," Terd answers from the bunk below. "Sometimes, this place feels like a prison. There are also rumors they have money problems. Cattle keep disappearing, and the banks about to take over the ranch."

"What do you mean cattle keep disappearing, I ask.

"Don't know. Nobody does. Just keep coming up short on the headcount. I heard they lost six last month and four the month before. So they may be roaming free and just haven't been found."

"Yeah," I reply, "I don't think they can wander too far with the security fence around this place."

"That's why they put up the fences and the cameras, or so they say."

"What about those cowboys in the chow hall? Can't they figure out how the cows are disappearing?"

"Cowboys?" Seth says, laughing. "We call them the 'prison guards.' They might be *wannabe* cowboys, but they ain't *real* cowboys. Most of them just ended up stayin' on here when they finished rehab."

"You mean everyone here's been through treatment?"

"I don't know about everyone," Todd replies, "but most the people work here for room and board. We work our asses off and don't get paid a cent. So they can't be hurtin' that bad. It ain't cheap to get in here, and they're all driving brand new trucks."

"Then why'd they turn it into a treatment center if it was such a successful ranch before?"

"They had a son named Kyle, Drew says. "Died eight years ago. One of the cafeteria ladies told me he got into the rodeo circuit a while back—rode bulls. He drew the meanest bull in Reno and got thrown. He broke his back, so he couldn't ride anymore, then got hooked on prescription painkillers.

"They tried everything—Alcoholics Anonymous (A.A.), Narcotics Anonymous (N.A.), rehabs, hospitals, everything—but he still couldn't get clean. They spent every dollar they had tryin' to save him, but in the end, he OD'd on opioids."

"Oh wow," I say, thinking maybe I judged Sue a little too quickly.

"That's why they turned this place into a treatment center," Drew continued. "Tryin' to help others with addictions get clean. Figure if they could have kept Kyle working here instead of joinin' the rodeo, he'd still be here."

"That's sad," I say, "but how is the bank taking the ranch if it's been in their family so long?"

"Rehab's expensive," Todd explains. So the Warden had to take out loans to pay for Kyle's treatment and used the ranch as collateral. Those loan collectors are ruthless when it comes to payin' off debts."

"What about the daughter I met earlier?"

"Vanessa?"

"I guess so. She didn't tell me her name."

"Vanessa is nice to look at, but she doesn't lift a finger around here."

"Who's this *Pit Bull* I keep hearing about?"

Drew's eyes get big. "You haven't met Pit Bull yet?"

"No," I say, "who's Pit Bull?"

"Well, the Warden runs the in-patient treatment program, or so they call it, but Pit Bull runs the ranch. He's what they call the Foreman. Probably the scariest person you'll ever meet—not just yellin' like Sue—I mean, real *mean* too. So watch out," he says. "You don't want to get into it with Pit Bull!"

Seth gets up, goes to the bathroom, and gets back in his bed. "My advice is just to do your time here and get away as soon as you can." His words hang in the air, and they sound familiar. Maybe that's because it's exactly what Kris told me less than 24 hours ago. A few minutes later, I hear Todd snoring in the bunk below.

I'm lying in bed, sleep the furthest thing from my mind, when I hear a board squeak on the steps outside. I'm about to get up and see who it is when I hear a "click."

"What was that?" I ask in a whisper.

"That's Sue. She's locking up," Drew says.

"What do you mean? We're locked in here at night?"

Seth laughs. "Wait for it…" he says, his voice climbing in anticipation.

"Wait for *what*?"

"Wait for it…" he says again, just before the lights in all four cabins go out at the same time.

"Welcome to Serenity Ranch," Seth replies as a dark stillness spreads across the valley.

CHAPTER 4

5:00 AM is an ungodly hour. It's one thing when you wake up early, say around 8:00 or 9:00 AM because your body and mind are well-rested. It's another when the guy in the bunk below you farts so loud it spooks the horses.

Terd is a mess. I tried calling him "Todd," but now that I've seen what the guy can do first-hand, "Todd" is no longer an appropriate name. I can sleep through someone snoring, but someone farting all night is impossible.

To be honest, we all farted throughout the night. We sounded like the brass section of a concert band. The worst part of it is that Terd sleeps on his stomach, his bunk is right below mine, and he plays them all—the trumpet, French horn, tuba, and bass trombone.

Here's an interesting fact—four people don't fit in one bathroom at the same time. There's not even time to brush your teeth after everyone takes a leak. But what's even worse is that Terd is in there almost 10 minutes and announces that the bathroom is condemned when he walks out. It's 5:20 in the morning, for crying out loud. (Who takes a crap at 5:20 in the morning?)

At 5:30, we all head up to the corral for morning chores. We look like the walking dead.

When we get to the corrals, a guy with a beard and a military haircut starts taking roll. "Cabin 1?"

"Here," yells someone to my right.

"Cabin 2?"

"H-here," Seth says, in the middle of a yawn.

"Cabin 3?"

"Everyone's here, except Donnie," yells someone in the back.

"Where's Donnie?"

"Chili last night gave him the shits."

"All right," the guy with the beard says, "but he still needs to be here for roll call. So tell him to come and find me before breakfast. I want to check him out myself. Cabin 4?"

"All here," sings a female voice to the left. I can't see her face because it's still dark outside, but I can't help but notice the melody in her voice. At least someone's excited to be up at this god-forsaken hour.

"All right, listen up, Same as yesterday…and the day before. Cabin 1's milking cows, Cabin 2's muckin' stalls, Cabin 3's feedin' cows, and Cabin 4's got eggs."

"Cabin 4's always got eggs!" Seth complains. "Why do they always get the easy job?"

The same female voice responds, but this time she isn't singing. "Those hens have daggers for claws, *dumbass*! Bring those chicken legs of yours over. If you think droppin' the soap in prison was bad, there's a chicken I want to introduce you to."

Laughter erupts from the group, even though no one is more than half-awake. I guess this is the start of a typical day at Serenity Ranch.

"Alright, alright. Take it easy," the guy with the beard says, "Let's help each other out. If your group finishes chores early, help another group out with theirs. Breakfast is at 7:00 so don't be late. And remember to clear your dishes. The next time someone leaves their tray on the table, you'll be washing dishes after evening chores."

Drew looks at me and asks, "You don't have boots?"

"No," I say, "just these," pointing to my Chuck Taylors with the rubber bands.

"Seth, you and Terd start movin' the horses into the corral. We'll catch up with you," he says.

The groups head off in separate directions, and Drew introduces me to the Army dude.

"This is Jake. He just got in last night. Jake, this is Mike. He's the parole officer."

I shake hands with the guy and realize he's one of us. "Welcome, Jake. Glad to meet ya."

"Parole officer?" I ask. "What's that?"

"It just means that he's in charge when none of the staff are around. Kind of like the class leader, right Mike?"

"Somethin' like that," Mike says, "I thought I was done with leadership when I got out of the Army. Anyway, what do you guys need?"

"Jake, here, needs some boots."

"What size ya' wear?" Mike asks

"Eleven or Eleven and a half."

"Follow me," he says as he leads me into a small barn next to the corrals. "Lucky for you, some guys leave their boots here when they finish. You can try all you like, but there's just no way to get some smells out of leather. It ain't a great selection, but there're some cowboy boots and some work boots in a pile over there. Grab a pair that fits. I'll find you some work gloves."

I rummage through the pile and find a pair I like. They are brand-new work boots, and they fit perfectly but have no shoelaces. (Imagine that!)

At the bottom of the pile, I find an old pair of cowboy boots that looks like they might have been left here by Lewis and Clark. Since I can't find anything else bigger than a size ten, I decide they'll have to do.

The first one goes on easy until I get my foot all the way in. That's when I discover that cowboy boots have no insoles or cushion whatsoever. I've never worn such uncomfortable shoes in all my life.

I start to pick up the other boot when a snake crawls out of it. I can't tell you what kind of snake it is because I don't stick around to find out. Instead, I run out of the barn with one boot on, the other in my hand, screaming like a little girl.

I run right into Mike and almost knock him on his back. "What the…?"

"Snake!" I yell, pointing to the barn.

"Okay, but do the boots fit?"

I drop the boot upside down to make sure there are no other surprises. Whether they fit or not is no longer my concern. There's no way I'm going back into that barn.

"They're perfect," I reply,

When I get back to the corrals, Seth, Terd, and Drew have moved the horses and are digging through the beds of straw, picking out clumps of horse poop.

"Grab a pitchfork and a shovel and help Terd in that next stall," Drew says, "we've only got two wheelbarrows."

We shovel so much poop for the next hour that I get a blister on my left hand. Unfortunately, with all the excitement in the barn, I forgot to get the work gloves from Mike.

We dump the manure, or "meadow muffins," as Terd calls them, into a composting stall. Then, without me asking, Terd explains the process of composting in exquisite detail.

He also tells me that an adult horse poops about eight times a day, equivalent to about 50 pounds, and that compost is good fertilizer around the garden. He also explains that dry meadow muffins can be used as firewood, although they are a little harder to light.

I swear the first thing I'm going to do when I get out of this place is apply to be a contestant on *Jeopardy*. Terd has an unlimited supply of useless knowledge in his brain, and I have a feeling I'm going to hear every word of it.

For the most part, 'mucking the corrals' isn't too tricky. First, we pick out the poop and shovel the straw that the horses' pee'd on into the composting pile. Once that's done, we spread fresh straw on the floor for new bedding (or is it hay? I can't remember the difference). Next, we sweep the alleyway between stalls and fill the water in the troughs (because adult horses drink up to 12 gallons of water a day—thanks, Terd!).

The last thing we do is fill the horses' feed buckets and move them back in their stalls. But, of course, as soon as they're back, they start pooping. How's that for gratitude?

Within minutes there's a steaming pile of poop in each of the stalls. It's like they have to make room for what they're about to eat. One down, seven to go. (And I guess maybe it's not too early in the morning to take a crap after all.)

Breakfast consists of buttermilk biscuits and gravy, thick strips of bacon, and skillet potatoes. I can feel my arteries clogging as I eat, and when I finish, I'm ready for a nap. But unfortunately, that's not going to happen.

At precisely 7:30 AM, we are back at the corrals waiting to find out what we'll be doing the rest of the day. The Parole Officer makes sure everyone has a pair of work gloves and a canteen filled with clean drinking water. I hear a pickup truck coming up the road, but I can't take my eyes off the beautiful countryside. I pull out a cigarette and light it while I stare at the mountains.

Just as the adrenaline from the snake episode finally fades out of my system, I hear—no, I *feel*—a gunshot right behind me. I nearly crap my pants for the second time today. One of the girls screams like she got shot, and Terd drops to his knees and starts crying. Even the horses are spooked, and a couple of them rear and buck in their stalls.

When I turn around, I see a guy with a pistol in his hand and a trail of white smoke coming out the barrel. (I thought that only happened in Hollywood movies, but then I haven't seen a lot of guns in our gated community.)

He's average height, probably just a couple inches shy of six feet, but stocky, with the build of a professional wrestler. He's wearing a buttoned-up western shirt that looks like it's two sizes too small, a pair of wrangler jeans that barely fit over his thighs, and a leather belt with a buckle only slightly smaller than the one worn by the current WWE Heavyweight Champion.

Before anyone has a chance to speak, he yells "git it," and a vicious-looking German Shepard leaps out of the back of the pickup truck and runs toward an area of tall grass about 30 feet away. He sniffs around and then darts into a bush.

When the dog comes back, he has a wounded rabbit in his mouth, dripping blood from a wound in his hind leg and screaming like a newborn baby. The dog trots over and drops the dying rabbit at the feet of the man with the gun and lies down.

"That was some shot, Pit Bull!" Seth says.

I think everyone else must be as shocked as I am because no one says a word. But, then, when the man bends down, picks up the bunny, and wrings its neck, Donnie, the kid with the shits, turns and pukes on my boots. (Can this day get any better?)

When the squealing fades away, the man looks at me and says, "We're eatin' rabbit stew tonight, boys."

Pit Bull tosses the rabbit in the back of the truck and puts the tailgate down. "Git in there," he says and closes the tailgate once the dog jumps in. The German Shepard pays the dead rabbit no attention and lies down on his stomach with his head resting on his front paws.

"Looks like we got a new inmate," Pit Bull says as he walks over, sizing me up the entire way. "You gotta name?"

"Jake," I reply.

"Hope you're ready to work, Jake, 'cause that's what we do here."

Pit Bull gives out the work assignments and somehow leaves me out. "What am I doing?" I ask, dreading what I think is coming.

"You'll see. Wait for me in the truck. I gotta talk to the parole officer a minute."

I once had a pit bull chase me up the main street in Issaquah. I was coming home from baseball practice and already late for dinner when he saw me and chased me several blocks. He was the meanest dog in town and probably would have eaten me if I hadn't climbed a tree.

I sat in that tree for two hours while he barked, and barked, and barked. I don't know if he had rabies or what, but he was drooling and foaming at the mouth.

I waited another 30 minutes after he got bored and left before I climbed down from that tree.

I get in the truck and wait for Pit Bull, just like he told me to do. If he's trying to let me know who's boss—it's working. I hate pit bulls.

* * * * *

Ten minutes later, we're pulling around the main lodge when Pit Bull turns to me and says, "See that lodge?"

"Yes, sir."

"You ain't got no business being in there, understand?"

"Yes, sir."

"The Hartwells live up there. You go anywhere near that house; you'll get a 1-minute head start before six hungry coon hounds are on your ass. And let me tell you something 'bout those hounds, boy," he says, looking over at me, "the only two things they eat are T-bones and testicles…and I don't see a lot of meat on you."

Pit Bull and I drive all the way back to Highway 2, mostly in silence. There's no telling where he might be taking me, and I'm too afraid to ask.

One thing I *do* know, however—I'd be just fine if he took me all the way back to Ellensburg. When we get to Highway 2, Pit Bull checks for oncoming traffic, and when it' clear, makes a right turn into the right lane.

The divided two-lane highway has a double-yellow line because of a downhill section behind us and a curve ahead of us. Another truck, not quite as big as the F350, comes around the bend heading toward us.

"Oh *shit!*" Pit Bull says as soon as he sees the truck.

"What is it?"

"That's Goodman's truck," he says, pointing to the Dodge Ram 2500 about a quarter-mile away.

We're still speeding up when the truck ahead veers into our lane. Pit Bull says something else, this time under his breath, but I don't have to hear it to know he's pissed. The truck is coming straight at us, and I'm sure we're about to die.

At the very last second, Pit Bull swerves onto the shoulder of the road, just as the truck flies by us with the driver hanging out the window, giving us the bird.

"What the hell was that?" I yell, still holding onto the door handle and bracing myself against the console between the front seats.

"An asshole!" Pit Bull replies as he brings the truck to a stop in the gravel on the side of the road.

"You know that guy?"

Pit Bull is in a rage and punches the middle of the steering wheel so hard that I think the airbag will deploy.

"Paul Goodman," he says. "Owns the ranch next to ours. He's been trying to buy it from us for years. Won't take 'no' for an answer."

"Why'd he just try to kill us?"

"Bad blood," he replies. "He's just trying to scare us, that's all."

"Well, he's doin' a hell of a good job at it," I confess, as Pit Bull puts it in drive and starts down the road again.

About three miles down the road, we see a large trailer transport pulling off the highway onto a road marked with a sign that says, "Chelan Custom Meats." Pit Bull slows the truck down and pulls off the road behind the semi-trailer. I can't tell what it's carrying, but from the smell, it's either cows or pigs or something dead.

We follow the big rig for maybe half a mile before turning into a parking lot for a meatpacking warehouse. There's a sign on it, just like the one at the intersection of Highway 2. Pit Bull drives around the back of the building just as the transport trailer comes around the other side. The truck backs up to a metal corral with an open gate and waits.

When Pit Bull parks the truck and turns off the engine, the reality of what I'm about to experience sets in. I'm tempted to stay right where I am, but I know how that will end, so I open the passenger door and get out.

It's now plain to see there are cows in the trailer because I can hear them mooing before we even get out of the truck. It appears that the trailer is full because all I can see are eyes and noses at every ventilation grate along the side. The air is tense, and I can feel the anxiety of the animals inside.

"What the hell is this place?" I ask.

"Where you'll be workin' today," Pit Bull replies. "They're a couple of hands short and need a young strapping boy like yourself."

"What am I going to be doing?"

Pit Bull starts to answer me just as the back door of the processing plant opens, and three men with rubber aprons and rubber boots walk out and head directly to the back of the trailer. They unlatch the ramp and let it down before opening the trailer door.

The first few cows meander down the ramp, their limbs stiff from the long ride. It isn't fast enough for the men, so they shock them with cattle prods delivering 4,000 volts of electricity. After that, the cows start running into the chute, having no idea what's coming next.

Once the first cow gets to the end of the chute, a gate closes behind her. The third man in a rubber apron takes something that looks like a nail gun, connected to a pneumatic hose, and pulls the trigger. A penetrating captive bolt punctures the cow's skull, rendering her unconscious and, supposedly, unable to feel pain.

She instantly falls to the ground but begins shaking violently. The man hits her a second time, and this time she stops moving as blood runs from her forehead.

Her lower legs are cut off with an electric saw, and she is hoisted onto a conveyor belt by a hook through a major tendon on one of her hind legs. From there, she enters the processing line, and a worker plunges a knife directly into her neck, severing her carotid artery. She dies moments later as every drop of blood drains from her body.

The remaining cows must have seen what just happened because they refuse to leave the trailer. The cattle prod changes their minds. After the first dozen exit the trailer, the other cows are blocked by a cow that fell during transport. She is either too weak, sick, or injured to walk. The men call this one a "downer," and she requires assistance to get out of the trailer.

That *'assistance'* comes in the form of a rope tied around her neck. The two men then drag her from the truck, down the ramp, and over concrete to the conveyor belt. At that point, she is stunned, hoisted, and "stuck" with the knife, all in less than a minute.

It feels as if I've also been struck with the penetrating captive bolt myself. I stand near the chute, completely speechless because I've never imagined such cruelty in all my life.

"C'mon," Pit Bull says, after the last cow bolts out of the trailer, "I'm gonna introduce you to Shane. You're workin' for him today. I'll be back at 4:30 to pick you up. Got it?"

"Wait! I'm working here all day?" I ask, praying I misunderstood what he just said.

"Don't worry, Jake, I've got a roast beef sandwich for you in the truck."

"Y-you think I'm going to eat a *roast beef* sandwich after seeing that?"

"Up to you," Pit Bull says as he walks off to find Shane.

When they return, Shane looks at me and says, "Yeah, he'll do."

"Alright, buddy," Pit Bull says, slapping Shane on the back. "If you have any trouble, give me a call." With that, he walks to the truck and starts to get in.

"Hold on," I yell, running to the truck. "You can't leave me here. I'm here for rehab. What the hell's going on?"

Pit Bull gets out of the truck and sticks his finger in my chest, pushing me back with the same force as a cattle prod.

"This *is* your rehab, dumbass! You've been too busy stickin' needles in your arm and snortin' drugs to learn how to work. My pa used to say, 'An idle mind is the playground of the devil,' and, boy, you gotta give that devil a break."

"You don't know me!" I yell back at him.

"You don't think so?" Pit Bull asks, "I've seen a hundred guys come through here exactly like you—laziest sons-of-bitches I've ever seen."

I can tell Pit Bull is just getting started. "Your ma and pa probably sent you off to a bunch of those head-shrinks thinkin' they'll help you get off of drugs, didn't they? What you *really* need is someone to kick you in the ass and show you what a day of hard work looks like."

"I'm not doin' it." I yell back, "You can't make me work here."

Pit Bull laughs. "Oh, Jakie-boy," he says, "that's where *you're* wrong. It's this or state prison—you know that! All I gotta do is make one phone call, and you'll be standing in front of that judge again by lunchtime. That what you want?"

"That's bullshit!" I say, "this is illegal. You can't make me work in a slaughterhouse."

"I can make you do whatever I damn well please. You don't get it, do you, Jake? Serenity Ranch ain't no drug treatment program—it's a prison *diversion* program. You came here to avoid a prison sentence, remember? So that means you participate in the *diversion* program, or you go to prison—how hard is that to understand?"

I look at Shane, who's just standing next to the trailer.

"What's it gonna be, Jake? Pit Bull asks. "You stayin' or leavin'? I've got work to do, so make up your mind."

He's right. I had a choice, and I chose to spend six months in a prison diversion program rather than a year in prison. I'm stuck here. Like I said before, there's no way I'm going back to jail.

I look back at Shane and ask, "What do you want me to do?"

"Just a little cleaning, Jake. That's all. I need you to spray out these trucks once they're unloaded and do the same inside once they finish butchering the cattle."

"I don't have to do any *killing?*"

"No," he laughs. "We're licensed by the U.S. Department of Agriculture. The employees who work directly with the cattle have to be trained and certified. Believe it or not, this is the *humane* way of butcherin' cattle, Jake. You don't want to see how some people do it out on their own. We're a government-licensed facility, operating under state laws."

"Okay," I reply, surrendering all remaining resistance. "Where do you want me to start?"

Just as Pit Bull starts to pull away, he stops and rolls down the window.

"Almost forgot. Here's your sandwich, Jake. I think his name was 'Homer.' Anyway, he's mighty delicious!" He tosses me a sandwich wrapped in plastic wrap and drives off, laughing all the way back to Highway 2.

For the next seven hours, I'm dressed in a rubber apron, rubber boots, rubber gloves, and a clear plastic face shield. I spend the rest of the morning hosing down the inside of the semi-trailers as they arrive, one after another. At times, two or three trucks are waiting their turn to unload cattle.

Scattered chunks of manure and runny puddles of diarrhea cover the deck of the trailers, disclosing just how long and difficult the transport must have been for these pitiful creatures. I counted as many as 23 heads of cattle packed into one trailer, and these aren't small dairy cows either. They are full-grown, adult beef cows fattened up on grain, corn, and barley.

In one trailer, two cows did not survive the trip. Most likely, they were either crushed or suffocated. Can you imagine being thrown around in a livestock mosh pit for eight or nine hours?

After the last delivery, Shane escorts me to the processing area. This is where the cows are delimbed, exsanguinated, skinned, decapitated, eviscerated, and dismembered. In other words, they get slaughtered. What comes out the other end no longer resembles a cow. Instead, it looks like something you'd find hanging in the back of the meat department at the local grocery store. There is blood from ceiling to floor, and the metallic smell makes me want to puke.

I hose down the entire processing line with a high-heat steam treatment, followed by a chemical detergent and a disinfecting solution of hydrogen peroxide and acetic acid. Fortunately, someone else takes care of the knives, blades, saws, and other machines. Since I can't be trusted with shoelaces, I probably shouldn't be around 10-inch boning knives or 14-inch scimitar blades.

When I finish, I clean up the best I can and walk outside to wait for Pit Bull. It's a little after 4:00 PM, and this is the first break I've had since 10:30 this morning. Even my cigarette tastes like a rusty nail. I've never felt more disgusting in all my life.

I've already decided that as soon as I get back to the ranch, I'm going to see Dr. Hartwell and tell him what I think of his prison diversion program. I'm not going to be some temp fill-in at the slaughterhouse every time they're short a custodian. I'm also not going to be part of some slave camp that takes orders from a narcissist like Pit Bull. He enjoyed putting me in my place this morning.

Pit Bull doesn't like how I smell when he picks me up, so I have to sit in the truck bed with the dog all the way back to the ranch. That's fine with me because I have nothing to say to Pit Bull, anyway.

Initially, I worried that the German Shepard would catch the scent of blood on me and start looking at me like I'm a T-bone steak. But the old dog just sits there with his eyes half open and his muzzle on his front paws, growling every time we hit a bump. He's not interested in me at all. I'm still wary of him, though, because even though he has grey around his muzzle, his teeth could shred my arm if he wanted to.

About a mile from the ranch, one of the bumps catapults me forward, and I find myself within striking distance of the big dog. But, to my surprise and disappointment, he doesn't try to eat me. Instead, he cowers down against the truck bed, whimpering like he's just been whipped.

Dogs his size shouldn't be afraid of people, especially ranch dogs who work alongside their owners all day long. I put my hand out a few inches to let him smell me and know that I'm not a threat. As my hand moves closer, he cowers ever further and growls in his throat.

"It's okay," I tell him again, "Don't be scared. I'm not going to hurt you." I begin to unwrap the sandwich I didn't eat for lunch, and his tail starts to wag involuntarily. "You want some of this, boy?"

I sit up very slowly and set the sandwich down about a foot from his nose and then return to my position on the other side of the truck.

He sniffs the sandwich and watches me. Then, when I push it closer to him, he slowly inches forward, picks it up in his mouth, and returns to the other side of the truck.

He gulps it down in two bites and looks back at me. His eyes are milky brown and soft, but I can sense there's some pain in there too. I tell myself that he's trying to say, 'thank you,' but he's probably just asking what I plan to do with the other half of the sandwich.

I put the other half in front of him because I have no intention of ever eating beef again. He gobbles that up and then lies back down, but this time a little bit closer than he was before, and his eyes are nearly closed.

* * * * *

Pit Bull stops the truck in front of the lodge, and I jump out. He pulls around to the corral, and as soon as he's out of sight, I head straight to the front door.

The door is as solid as the tall pines from which it's made, and no one hears my knock. It's dangerous to walk into someone's house unannounced. I walked into a friend's house without knocking once and almost got killed. He thought it was a drug bust and fired four shots through the bathroom door.

After several moments pass, I push the door open and call out, "Hello. Is anyone home?"

I'm standing in a gathering room built for dining and entertaining. The room opens into a cathedral ceiling. Two giant cedar poles extend from the ground level up to the roof structure three floors above.

The hardwood floors and cedar walls give the lodge a rustic feel. However, the leather furniture, freestanding fireplace, and live-edge dining table cut from Maple Burl give it a modern look. If the Hartwells are having financial difficulty, they hide it quite well.

Two connecting hallways off the main room lead to opposite ends of the house. I can't see what's down the hallways, but I imagine they lead to bedrooms, bathrooms, closets, and other rooms you'd typically find in someone's private residence.

I am awe-struck by the view of the mountains and lake through large plate-glass windows on the front and the back of the house. It is nearly a panoramic view of the entire valley. I've seen some fabulous homes in my life, and this is no exception.

"Hello," I call again, listening to the echo repeat itself down the hallways. It feels like I am entirely alone in the house until I hear footsteps coming down one of the upstairs hallways.

Vanessa appears on the landing of the second floor. "Hello Jacob," she says, "how nice to see you again."

Her hair is wet, and she's wearing a sleek bathrobe and slippers. "I was just getting a shower and didn't hear you come in."

"I'm looking for Dr. Hartwell," I reply, getting nervous as she starts down a set of stairs toward me. "I need to speak to him."

"I'm afraid he's not well," she says. "He's in his bedroom sleeping right now. Is there something I can do for you?"

"Uh, no, I don't think so. I just need to talk to him about a few things."

"I'll let him know you came by. Are you sure there isn't *anything* I can do for you?"

The tone of her voice leaves no question as to what's on her mind, but the only two things on my mind are to speak with Dr. Hartwell and take a long shower—alone.

On my way to the cabin, I see another pretty girl, this one with long, dark hair sitting on the pier, writing in a book. She waves to me, and I wave back. She doesn't intimidate me like Vanessa does. If I didn't have so much on my mind, I'd go over and talk to her. But then again, I smell like a meat locker.

When I get back to the cabin, everyone is already at chow or doing chores, so I take off the clothes I'm wearing and set them outside. I'll have to remember to do something with them later. Otherwise, they'll attract bears, and this place is dangerous enough as it is.

I stand in the shower for nearly ten minutes, doing nothing more than letting the hot water run down the length of my body. Getting clean feels good and helps calm me down.

When I walk back outside, the girl with the book I saw is climbing up the path from the lake. We make eye contact again, and this time she walks right up to me.

"Hi, I'm Erika." As soon as she starts speaking, I recognize she's the girl with the beautiful voice who scolded Seth for complaining this morning.

"Hey, Erika, I'm Jake."

"I know, she says, "I heard The Warden introduce you last night."

"Oh, right. I forgot about that." How long have you been here?"

"About…six weeks, I guess. They sent me here after I got my second DUI a couple of months back."

"Did you do any in-patient time or just come straight here?"

"I didn't have to go to a hospital if that's what you mean. The judge sent me here because he knows Dr. Hartwell and thought this would be a good place for me to 'grow up and take responsibility for my actions.'"

"Is it?"

"Yeah, I guess so. I've certainly learned to appreciate how easy my life was before I came here."

"What about the treatment?"

"Treatment? There really isn't any," she says. "We hold meetings because there are people who are really trying to get off drugs, but it's not like we're learning any coping skills to deal with our problems or anything."

"That's strange," I say, "I've been in treatment centers where all you do is have group meetings and behavioral therapy classes all day. I've never seen a place that just makes you work and calls that therapy."

"Yeah, I know. It is strange, not that I have much experience with rehab, but I don't think I'm learning how to live without drugs and alcohol, you know?"

"Where are you from?"

"Vancouver. The one near Portland. And you?"

"I'm from Issaquah. Do you know where that is?"

"I know exactly where it is. Tiger Mountain is one of my favorite trails."

"No way! You know Tiger Mountain? I used to hike there all the time and watch people fly paragliders from the top. "

"Yeah, it's a great trail," she says. "I run trail marathons, and that's one of my favorite places to train."

"Wait. You run marathons in the mountains?"

"Yeah, lots of people do."

"Wow!" I respond. "And I thought 26.2 miles on flat roads was challenging enough."

Actually," she says, "most trail marathons are *ultramarathons*, meaning they're longer than a normal marathon."

I don't know what to say to that. Every time I run a marathon, I feel like I'll die before reaching the finish line.

"Hey, our cabin is tending to the horses for evening chores. You want to come along?"

"Sure," I say. "I was just headed up to find Drew, Seth, and Terd…I mean Todd. Maybe I'll find them up there."

Erika laughs, which I find intoxicating. "Oh, Terd is right," she says. "His reputation precedes him—especially if you're standing downwind. Actually, I think he may have a medical condition."

We laugh all the way up to the barn, where she introduces me to Monica and Shelby. Monica's six months are almost up, and she's going back to Spokane in a couple of weeks.

"You must be excited to get back home."

"Not really," she says, "in fact, I may stay in Cashmere for a while. It's just a little west of here. I have some friends that I met here, and they're all living in a sober house together."

"What about your family back home? Don't you want to see them?"

"I've been on my own for a while. My family isn't exactly supportive of me. Besides, I've kind of got a new family now."

Shelby stops brushing one of the horses and says, "She has a boyfriend. She's waiting for him to get out of here so they can get married."

"Wait a second. You met someone in treatment, and the two of you are getting married?"

"Yeah?" Monica says as if it were the stupidest question she's ever heard.

"I know it's none of my business, but how long have you known each other?"

"Three months. Why?"

"You don't think that's a little fast? I mean, seriously, how *well* do you know him?"

"Long enough to know that we love each other," she says, "and we'll be able to help each other stay in recovery."

There are a hundred more questions I'd like to ask, but Erika gives me a look that says it's none of my business.

"Well, I hope everything works out well for you guys," I say. "You'll have to introduce me to him sometime. I'd really like to meet him."

Monica giggles and says, "You already have. He's your bunkmate in Cabin 2."

* * * * *

When I finally find Drew, Seth, and Terd, my head is still spinning. I hear a truck pull up behind me, hauling a flatbed trailer. Drew steps out of the driver's side of the truck, and Seth and Terd jump down out of the pickup's bed.

Drew runs over and says, "Dude! How was your first day?"

"I'm still here, aren't I?"

Drew laughs, "Yeah, we had a bet going on that. Terd and Seth each owe me five bucks. I knew as soon as we met, you're not a quitter."

Terd walks over and gives me a big hug. "I'm glad you're still here. I like having someone else on my side of the room. My older brother and I used to have bunk beds," he continues, "but my mom got rid of them after I fell out and landed on my head. She took me to the emergency room with a concussion. Hey, did you guys know there are approximately 36,000 bunk bed-related injuries each year…."

I have to cut Terd off, or his story may go on forever. "I didn't know that, Todd, but it sure does explain a lot."

I still can't call him "Terd" to his face. My mother taught me not to make fun of mentally challenged people, and I get the feeling Todd is a couple of geese short of a gaggle.

Drew puts the brooms away and walks out of the barn. "C'mon, you guys. We're on our own time now. I'm going for a swim in the lake. Anyone want to join me?"

*****

By the time the others get back from their swim, I've got all my t-shirts folded in six-inch squares. It's monotonous, but I think I know why Sue makes us do it. I once heard a decorated Navy Seal say that if you want to make a difference in the world, start by making your bed. He said if you can't do the little things right, you'll never get the big things right.'[2]

After everyone has had a turn in the shower, I've described my first day on the ranch several times already. None of them are surprised. In fact, it turns out that *everyone* gets that same introduction to the ranch—it's some sort of initiation or ritual Pit Bull does with the new people. It makes me mad that nobody warned me, but then again, nobody wants Pit Bull on their *ass*.

When I try to sleep tonight, I'll have nightmares of headless cows—that much I expect. What surprises me is that this is what they think helps addicts get clean.

"So, there is no treatment program here at all? I ask.

"Not like we're used to," Seth says. "But I'll be the first to admit that when I'm out there working or on the back of a horse, I never think about using drugs."

"Me too," Terd confesses. "I've never gone this long without having to be on Methadone. That's the only way I've ever been able to get off heroin before this."

"So, there aren't any 12-step meetings like in A.A. or N.A.?"

"Oh sure," Drew says. "We have them three times a week, but they're informal meetings. They're not mandatory. Anybody who wants to get together comes over here, and we hold a meeting from 7:00 to 8:00 PM, every other night. In fact," he says, "we have one tonight. You can join us."

"Thanks," I reply, "but I've been to enough of those meetings. I don't get a thing out of them."

"Suit yourself," Drew says, "if you change your mind, you're always welcome to join us."

At 7:00 PM, four others come over from various cabins, and Seth leads a meeting. It doesn't surprise me that one of them is Monica and that she sits very close to him.

---

[2] McRaven, William H., Make Your Bed: Little Things That Can Change Your Life…And Maybe The World, (New York, Grand Central Publishing, 2017), pg. 3.

Anyway, I'm still pissed about having to work in the slaughterhouse. So I put my earbuds in, lay back on my bunk, and listen to music for the rest of the night.

CHAPTER 5

After chores and breakfast the following day, I'm back in the truck again with Pit Bull. Fortunately, however, we're staying on the ranch today, and he's taking me on a tour of the work sites. The first is an emerald-green alfalfa field where Drew, Seth, and Terd are moving irrigation pipes.

We're sitting in the cab of the truck while Pit Bull gives me instructions. "Moving pipe is simple," he explains, "even an addict can do it. All you gotta do is disassemble the long line of aluminum pipe sections, move them, to the next water valve, at the top of the field and reconnect 'em."

Each section looks like it's about 20-feet long and has a smaller pipe extending off one end with a sprinkler on it. By the way that Terd is struggling to lift them, I'd say they weigh about 60 to 70 pounds apiece.

"When you've carried the pipe to the new line," he continues, "You make sure they're lined up straight and then stick the male end in the female end and give it a tug straight back. If the lines ain't straight, there'll be a water leak at the fittin' point."

"Once you got 'em connected again, you turn the water back on. It runs for a couple of hours, and then someone comes around and turns it off. Got it?"

"Sure," I reply, having already figured things out by watching Drew and Terd for about half as long as it took Pit Bull to explain it.

"See, I told you even an addict can do it," laughing a second time at his own stupid joke.

Drew and Terd are working on the ends of the line, while Seth works in the middle. Drew must have grown up on a farm because it takes him only a minute to carry a section of pipe to its new location, assemble it and walk back to get another pipe. Seth isn't quite as fast as Drew, but he's not too far behind. I don't think Seth grew up on a ranch, but he does know how to do it pretty quickly.

Terd, on the other hand, must have grown up on Mars, where scientists are still trying to figure out if water once existed. He can't figure out how to reconnect a pipe without setting it down and pushing it from the sprinkler end. Half the time, they don't line up straight, and he has to walk to the other end of the section and line them up again.

Aside from moving the pipe, each of them has an additional responsibility or two. Drew's job is to turn the water on, and he and Seth make sure everything is working correctly down the line. If it is, and there are no leaks, they move on to the next line.

Terd's job, on the other hand, is to walk down the field to the following line and pull the plug at the end so that the water can drain. Once that's done, he starts working back up the line, disconnecting pipe sections, and moving them to the next water line.

The only problem is that Terd was busy calculating the speed and rotational forces on Mars and forgot to replace the plug at the end of the previous line. Drew turns the water on and waits, but the sprinklers aren't spraying. He checks to make sure he turned the valve in the right direction, which he did, then realizes the problem and turns the water off.

Drew and Seth jump up and down at the top of the field and yell to get Terd's attention. Terd, however, is now designing a soil-sampling device in his head to end the water debate once and for all. But, no matter what they do, neither of them can get Terd's attention.

Pit Bull's been around long enough to know what's happening, so we drive down to the end of the faulty line. Pit Bull finds the plug right where Terd left it when he drained the last line. It ends up being a good opportunity for me to see how the fittings attach, but I have no doubt Terd's getting an ass-kicking from Pit Bull later on.

Pit Bull waves to Drew at the top of the field, letting him know he can turn the water back on. Instantly, the irrigation line comes to life and begins watering the alfalfa. Terd is still working his way up the other line, oblivious to his mistake.

Our next stop is to see how Cabin 3 is doing. They're supposed to be rounding up a small herd of cows that broke through a barbed-wire fence during the night. I heard that they took several hay bales out to the pasture this morning only to find the cows disappeared. They found most of them down by the reservoir grazing on lush, green grass, but one cow and her calf are still missing.

Two prison guards are on horses keeping the cows from wandering off while the others mend the fence. It takes several hands to replace the broken post, splice the severed ends, and stretch the wire using a prybar, wire cutters, and brute force. The girls from Cabin 4 are out with another prison guard looking for the cow and her calf, but it's mid-morning, and they're still searching.

Pit Bull checks with the prison guards to see if any cows are injured while I watch the repairs. I can see that the broken post is pretty old, but I'm surprised a cow could, or would, knock it down just to get to greener grass. It's not like they're starving or anything. Once Pit Bull's satisfied, we head out looking for the missing cattle.

"How do you think the cows got loose?" I ask.

"They probably found a loose post and worked on it 'til it busted."

"A cow could do that?" I ask. "Wouldn't they get cut on the wire?"

"Maybe," Pit Bull says, spitting tobacco juice into a red Solo cup. "Some of them cows are tippin' the scales at 1,500 pounds. You'd be surprised what they can do."

"Were any of them injured?"

"Didn't see none," he says, his eyes searching for any sign of the cow and her calf.

I'm quiet for a moment because he didn't answer my earlier question, so I ask it again. "Wouldn't they get injured on the barbed wire, though?"

Pit Bull looks over at me as we bounce down the dirt road and says, "See them leather gloves you got there? What do you think they're made of? *Cotton candy*? Them cowhides are tough. You get on the wrong side of one of them cows, and you'll find out just how dangerous those barbed-wire fences can be. Besides, you need to be looking for them other two cows that are still out there, not worrying about how the cows got loose."

I can tell Pit Bull isn't in the mood to discuss bovine behavior, so I stop asking questions. A few minutes later, I hear him say, "Oh, *shit*!" and slam on the brakes.

Pit Bull's out of the truck and running through the alfalfa field to a cow lying on her side. The field looks exactly like the one where Drew and Terd were just working, but I don't see any irrigation lines.

"Get over here, Jake!" Pit Bull yells as he drops to his knees in front of the cow.

I don't understand why the cow is lying on her side until I'm standing over her. The first thing I notice is how fat she is. The second is how much distress she is in. Her neck is extended, she's spewing white foam, her tongue is hanging out, and it sounds like she's suffocating.

"Is she pregnant?" I ask, not realizing her calf is less than six months old.

"She's got bloat!" Pit Bull says as he pulls a knife with a six-inch blade from the sheath on his belt. "Get down here and hold her still."

I'm barely on my knees, still trying to figure out how you hold a 1,500-pound cow still when Pit Bull plunges the knife into her side. Like a pinata, her abdomen explodes into a fountain of gas, fluid, and a green ooze made of partially digested alfalfa and saliva.

Unfortunately for me, I'm in the direct path of the rumen discharge, and it hits me squarely in the face. I fall on my back, covered in what seconds before were the contents of her stomach.

Because I'm on my back and trying to breathe at the same time, I inhale the vilest fluid I've ever tasted and immediately throw up all over my chest. Then, instinctively, I roll onto my stomach so as not to choke on my own vomit and look up at Pit Bull through the sputum dangling from my eyelashes.

"Sorry 'bout that," he says, without an ounce of compassion in his voice.

The release of the gasses has taken the pressure off the cow's lungs. She's breathing normally again. I, on the other hand, am not. I have absolutely no idea what I should do next, so I just sit there, with my head in my hands, feeling just as pitiful as I look.

The only thing I can think to ask is, "She gonna be okay?"

"Should be," Pit Bull says, pulling a handkerchief from his back pocket. He stuffs it into the wound and looks up at me, realizing what a mess I'm in. He tells me there's a blanket I can use in the truck, but I decline. At this point, it's best to man up and accept the situation without complaining. I calmly take off my shirt and use it to clean off my face.

Pit Bull gets on the radio, announces that we've found the cow, and gives the prison guards our location. He asks Sue to call the veterinarian because he doesn't have the supplies to clean and suture the wound.

"I've got to keep pressure on this," he says when he puts down the radio. "Go find that calf. It's probably already dead, but we've got to get it before the wolves do."

It doesn't take me long to locate the missing calf. Pit Bull was right—he is already dead. He wasn't but 20 yards away from his mother, and she probably heard him take his last toiled breath.

At six months old, this calf weighs more than 600 pounds (I know because Terd gives me the formula for estimating a cow's weight using an average birth weight of 80 pounds and a 3-pound gain per day, or 80 pounds+(180 days x 3 pounds per day) = 620 pounds).

My point is, I can't lift her, so I walk back to Pit Bull and tell him the news. He's on the radio again and tells the prison guards to bring a truck and trailer to pick up the calf. While we're waiting for the veterinarian and the prison guards, Pit Bull explains what "bloat" is.

Bloat occurs when a cow (or a sheep, goat, or horse) eats too much green forage (like alfalfa) and not enough roughages (such as hay). As a result, fermentation gases build up in the rumen, which is the first section of the stomach and the primary site where microbial fermentation of food occurs. In other words, the cow gets abdominal distension because it eats, at least in this case, too much alfalfa and not enough hay.

I sit in the bed of the truck on the ride back because, for the second day in a row, Pit Bull doesn't like the way I smell. It's becoming my regular seat. Besides, I don't feel like trying to make conversation with Pit Bull at this point. I'm still trying to digest—no, *process*—everything that's happened. I welcome the silence.

The German Shepard doesn't ask too many questions on the way back, but he keeps one eye on me as he slumbers in his usual spot near the cab. He's a good companion when you just need a little time to yourself.

I've never owned a dog, but if I did, this is the kind of dog I'd want. I can tell that he loves his master, even though his apprehension tells me that he's not treated very kindly in return.

We had an elderly neighbor in Issaquah whose best friend was a black and white Border Collie. But, unfortunately, his wife had already passed away, so it was just the old man and his dog.

That dog followed him everywhere. He rode in the passenger seat when they went out in the car and slept next to the old man's feet when he rocked in a chair on the veranda. Whenever they walked to the supermarket down the street, that dog sat just outside the front door until the old man came out and then followed him back home.

When the old man passed away, that dog's heart broke in two. He was all alone for the first time in his entire life. The old man's son lived across town, and they took him home, but it wasn't two days before that collie was back at the house looking for his best friend.

Sometimes, I'd come out of the grocery store, and he'd be lying there waiting to see if the old man was going to walk out and take him home. I tried to get him to follow me home a couple of times, but he never would.

Sometimes, I wonder what happened to that dog. People say that 'a dog is a man's best friend,' but I don't think you can say as often that 'a man is a dog's best friend.' If there is a heaven, I hope dogs get to be with their owners. (Unless their owner is Pit Bull.)

When we get back to the cabins, I jump out of the truck and head for the shower. But, before I get three paces from the vehicle, Pit Bull rolls down his window and sticks out his head.

"I saw you talkin' to that girl yesterday, Erika. Don't be getting' no ideas about her—she ain't interested in no *city* boy. If she's gonna be with anyone, she's gonna be with me. Ya hear?"

I walk to the cabin without turning around or saying a word. I just need to get through these next six months without getting myself killed. You'd think it wouldn't be that hard, right? But then again, I'm also an addict, and we have a way of making life way more complicated than it needs to be.

* * * * *

I'm sitting alone at dinner because Seth sits by Monica, and Terd and Drew aren't back from running into town with Sue. They needed a new chainsaw blade, and the store is in Wenatchee—a 50-minute drive each way.

Erika sets her tray on the table across from me and asks, "Mind if I join you?"

"No, have a seat," I reply, trying to hide a little of the excitement in my voice.

"Heard you've had a rough couple of days."

"Well," I begin, as she sits down and starts to butter a crescent roll. "Only if you call 'being interrogated, strip-searched, chased by a snake, shoveled horse poop, cleaned a slaughterhouse, shot in the face with cow puke, and thrown-up on myself' a rough couple of days, then yeah, I guess so."

She laughs and says, "Oh, so just like any other typical day around here, right?"

I motion over to Seth and Monica and say, "I didn't think you could date other patients in programs like this. At least not any that I've been a part of."

"Well, this isn't like any other program you've been part of, is it?"

"No. Not so far."

"They don't consider us patients here. We're like hired help that they don't have to pay—basically—free labor.

"Do you have a boyfriend?" I ask, surprising myself with my forwardness.

She laughs again. "No. I didn't come here looking for love. In fact, you're one of the only guys I've talked to since I've been here."

"Oh, I'm sure that's not true. I'll bet you get plenty of attention. What's the ratio? Something like four guys to every one girl?"

"They aren't my type."

I'm about to ask her what her type of guy is when Pit Bull walks in and sees Erika and me sitting together. He's not happy seeing us together, so instead of eating lunch, he turns around, slams the door, starts the truck, and peels out as he drives away.

"I'd better get back to my usual table," Erika says, like a Jedi sensing a disturbance in the force.

"Yeah," I sigh, "we don't want to upset the natural balance of things, now do we?"

She smiles at me as she picks up her tray. "Hey, I'm thinking about coming to a meeting tonight. You gonna be there?"

"Of course," I reply before I even realize what I'm saying.

"Great! See you there."

* * * * *

It's common for addicts to share their stories about addiction with one another. It doesn't matter how different our backgrounds may be—powerlessness over our addictions is common ground. Of course, we don't like talking to anyone *else* about our past, especially psychiatrists, caseworkers, and spouses, but when we're in a room with others suffering the devastating effects of addiction, we can relate to one another because of our shared experiences.

Monica is sitting next to Seth, Drew and Terd are next to them (though they aren't a couple, as far as I know), then it's Erika, Shelby, a guy named Vincent that I've never spoken to, and me.

Since this is Vincent's first 12-step meeting, we all take turns sharing our stories about addiction and how drugs and alcohol screwed up our lives. It's called a Step 1 meeting and, if you've never been to one, it can be quite a humbling experience.

I had no idea Seth was in the Army and got kicked out for using drugs. He only served three years, but he did a tour in Iraq, and when he came home, he was a completely different person. He was diagnosed with post-traumatic stress disorder, or PTSD, after sustaining injuries in a ballistic missile attack by Taliban forces outside the base.

He suffered a traumatic brain injury, and the Army would've medically discharged him, but because he got hooked on prescription pain killers, the Army dishonorably discharged him. Since he did not receive an honorable discharge, he lost all medical benefits for injuries he sustained defending America overseas. I don't know about you, but that doesn't seem right to me.

Seth didn't say too much about his time in Iraq, but it's obvious he came home with many physical and emotional wounds, which have still not healed. He can't hold a steady job, and he still wakes up with headaches and nightmares that he's back in Iraq. So it doesn't surprise me that he, and many others like him, turn to drugs to ease the pain.

Terd is a different story. I'm positive he has an IQ north of 160, which puts him in the exceptionally gifted club, but he got into trouble because he lacks basic social skills.

It's not that Terd *can't* make friends, but he doesn't seem to keep them very long. In the short time I've known him, I've noticed that he interrupts people when they're talking and has difficulty staying on topic. It's also hard for him to see things from other people's points of view. I'm not trying to find faults with the guy. I'm just sharing my observations.

Nate had some of the same behavioral issues, and because of that, I know that Terd doesn't do it on purpose. But, unfortunately, not everyone understands why he does socially unacceptable things—they just assume he's either anti-social or stupid.

As a result of the way some people treat him, Terd has low self-esteem. He got into drugs in high school because the only group that accepted him was the "stoners" or "potheads"—everyone else picked on him because he was different. He says that when he gets high, he feels more normal than ever before, and kids don't pick on him.

His difficulties arose when he flunked out of high school despite being the smartest kid in his class. Initially, he quit turning in school assignments, then started skipping classes, then stopped going to school altogether. Finally, he ended up living on the streets of Portland until the cops arrested him for breaking into someone's house. He said that he needed money to feed his habit.

As far as his D-O-C, what started with smoking a little weed became a full-fledged heroin addiction. After that, he discovered crystal meth and would probably already be dead if he were still on the streets. It's a heartbreaking story—and one I've heard countless times.

I'm the next to share my story, but I've told it a hundred times, so it's not hard for me to talk about it. It's your run-of-the-mill story about trying to deaden the pain of losing someone. I started using drugs not long after Nate died, and I've been in and out of treatment centers for the last six years.

* * * * *

The first time I ever tasted alcohol started as an innocent teenage stunt. But, unfortunately, it ended like a train wreck.

Unlike most high schools, Bellevue doesn't have a ski club, gaming club, or skateboarding club. According to the faculty administration and the board of directors, those organizations do nothing to prepare students for higher education or professional careers. Therefore, they are a waste of time.

No, Bellevue High School has *proper* clubs— physics, chemistry, real estate investment, that sort of thing. We even have a Student Organization for Cancer Research. That's right, I'm talking about after-school clubs for teenagers, but not the kind that brings people together to entertain or fill one's time. Instead, I'm talking about associations and societies designed to further one's passion for volunteerism, increase knowledge in a particular field of study, and generate professional career contacts. That's our definition of a "club."

My parents wanted me to join the mock trial club because I frequently argued with them. They never bothered to ask me if I had any interest in being an attorney. So instead, I ran for Student Body Vice President and won because I was popular.

Anyway, my point is that I didn't get to pick what kind of "club" I joined—I was automatically enrolled in ASB Leadership. Later, when I found out my father paid someone to rig the election, we had a huge blowup, and I quit the following day.

Our activity at the end of the fall term was an organized ski trip. The ASB Leadership faculty advisor was an avid skier and thought it would be fun to organize a trip to Crystal Mountain. It was supposed to be some kind of reward for all our hard work. After all, our math club had several members win medals in the USA Mathematical Olympiad. Additionally, two of our classmates competed on the national team that won the International Math Olympiad.

Our ASB Historian that year was Dillon Miller—a real clown. He thought it would be fun to sneak a bottle of his father's Glenfiddich scotch whiskey on the bus.

I didn't know anything about scotch whiskey or any other kind of alcohol, but I'd seen my father pour something over ice and sip it on special occasions. That, after all, was what his father did. On the other hand, my mother preferred wine and was more apt to drink on somewhat *less than* special occasions—because that's what her mother did.

We passed the bottle around, each taking a nip each time we rode the gondola up the mountain. I remember how it burned in my throat and then burned some more in my stomach. It was freezing outside, but I felt warm all over.

I loved that euphoric feeling that radiated through my body once the alcohol hit my brain. The more I drank, the better I felt. Even then, I didn't understand how to drink socially—I drank to get drunk.

Each ride up the mountain took about 30 minutes by gondola and another 30 minutes to ski back down. The three of us spaced the drinks pretty well throughout the afternoon. Sure, we got drunk, but we were just having fun, and nobody got hurt. But on the way back home, reclining in the soft leather seats in the back of the rented motor carriage, we finished the bottle.

For the first hour, I watched the lights of passing cars dance across the window, and it felt like the bus was in a constant left-hand turn. Soon, I began to feel sick and stumbled to the bathroom.

I remember throwing up in the toilet until there was nothing left in my stomach. I then threw up some more. I wanted to go back to my seat, but I knew I'd never make it in that condition and sat there until I passed out.

We'd all planned on sleeping over at Dillon's house, but I woke up the following day in my own bed. Someone had to have helped me out of that bathroom, off the bus, and into a car. Whoever helped me also carried me out of the car and put me in my bed.

I had no idea who it was that helped me, but neither did I ask. I was too embarrassed about getting that drunk. In fact, I never spoke to anyone about it—I just pretended it never happened. I think it might have been Dillon's father, or maybe his older brother, but someone got me back home and was either too embarrassed for me to tell me or didn't want to make a big deal about it.

What I did know from my first experience with alcohol was that I loved the feeling of being intoxicated. Later on, even when I knew there would be consequences for my drinking, I never left a glass or a bottle half-empty. I drink whatever is put in front of me, and I always drink to get drunk.

The first time I tried drugs was a completely different story. I'd felt the effects of alcohol and wanted more. I was at a friend's house a few months after Nate died and, emotionally, I was in a downward spiral. There was this giant hole in my heart, and I was tired of hurting.

My friend's name was Steven, although he was more of a "Stevie" than a "Steven." He was always joking around. I didn't even take him seriously when he asked me if I wanted to smoke some weed.

At first, I laughed and said, "You don't have any weed."

"Yeah, I do. My mom smokes it when my dad's out of town. She keeps it in her golf bag out in the garage. Doesn't think anyone knows about it."

"Aren't you afraid she'll find out?

"No way. She'll never notice it's gone. Besides, she smoked some with my sister the other night. I saw them sitting in the dark on the terrace when I got home."

"You're sisters like twenty, right? You're fifteen!"

"She's nineteen, and I'm sixteen! What's your problem anyway? You scared?"

"I'm not scared." I lied. "I just don't wanna get caught."

Stevie put one of the joints between his lips and handed me the other. "Stop being a pussy," he said, lighting his joint and tossing the lighter to me.

I was terrified of getting caught, but I also ached for the pain to go away. My grades were falling, and I couldn't sleep at night.

At the time, I was still talking to my parents, but I didn't say anything to them because they were having a difficult time themselves. They were fighting most of the time and, since they didn't notice that I was in a state of deep depression, I didn't tell them.

That union of flame and marijuana transformed my world. Stevie told me to slow down when I started inhaling it like it was my only oxygen source, but after that first tingle touched my brain, I felt like I was on a different planet. I've never truly returned to Earth.

The problem with my story is that it just keeps getting longer. No one believes this is my fifth time in rehab, that I've been arrested three times, gone to jail twice, and that I haven't died from all the drugs I've done. But, to be honest, it surprises me too.

For most people, addiction occurs after repeated exposure to an addictive stimulus to the point where a psychological or physiological dependence develops. It's often this way with people who drink coffee every morning or smoke cigarettes. But I'm not like most people. Addiction is in my DNA—I'm hooked the very first time I try it.

CHAPTER 6

We're taking a short water break when Pit Bull drives up. The German Shepard sits in the bed of the truck, waiting for his next command.

"Why ain't you guys workin'?

"C'mon, Pit Bull," Drew says, "we've been working all morning. We're just takin' a water break. It's freakin' hot out here."

Pit Bull walks up to Drew and puts a finger in his face. "You wanna see hot? How about I take you down to the slaughterhouse and let you work down there for the afternoon? You guys are slower than molasses!"

"Actually," Terd says, "moles can dig about 15 feet a day. So that's pretty good if you ask me."

"I *didn't* ask you, Terd," Pit Bull barks. "I'm talking about 'molasses,' you know? The kind you put on flapjacks. Not '*mole-asses*,' you idiot.

"Oh, sorry," Terd says, "I misunderstood."

"Well, then let me put this a different way. If you guys ain't done by the time I bring Jake back here, you'll be cleanin' chicken coops every day for the rest of your lives, you hear me?"

"Where am I going?" I ask.

"We need to ride up and check on a cow. Get in the truck."

"Can I finish this line first? There are just a couple more pipes to move, and we'll be finished with this field."

"Boy," Pit Bull yells, "Get your ass in that truck before I put a boot in it."

I'm sitting in the back of the truck in a cloud of dust, trying not to get close to the German Shepard. He's lying near the cab, growling every time we hit a bump.

At least I have a choice this time. I can sit up front with Pit Bull or ride in the back with the German Shepard. However, it's an easy choice—I prefer the company in the back.

This time he doesn't growl when I get in the truck. In fact, he wags his tail, and I'm pretty sure he smiled at me. Unfortunately, I don't have anything to feed him, but I'll remember to grab something for him from the chow hall at lunch.

I haven't seen Pit Bull since he stormed out of the chow hall a few nights ago. Hopefully, he's forgotten about Erika and me sitting together. Maybe he's had some time to think about it, and he's either gotten over it or decided not to pursue it. Anyway, I'd rather be sitting back here with a German Shepard than upfront with a Pit Bull.

It's a beautiful day in central Washington, and things are looking up for the first time in a while. I'm starting to get the feel of this place, and the work isn't all that bad. I've even been able to make some good friends along the way.

It also feels good to wake up sober in the morning and not be scratching an itch that doesn't go away or planning my day around when and where I can score some drugs. That gets old really fast!

People don't understand how debilitating an addiction can be. I knew I had a problem with alcohol when I'd wake up in the morning with a hangover, and my first thought was to have another beer.

They call that "the hair of the dog that bit you." The phrase originated from the medieval belief that the burnt hair from a dog was an effective antidote against the effect of the dog's bite. In drinking circles, it means that the best thing for a hangover is another drink.

When the first thing I wanted to do in the morning was get a buzz on, I knew I had a problem. That *problem* progressed to the point that I soon had to have a drink in the morning just to function properly and several more throughout the day.

Let's put it this way—have you ever woken up in the morning and said, "if I don't have a drink, there's no way I can drive myself to school or work?" If you have—you're an alcoholic.

If you are addicted to drugs, heroin, and meth in particular, but any drug (including alcohol), you become so preoccupied with getting high that nothing else matters. Jobs don't matter. Families don't matter. Debt doesn't matter. Jail doesn't even matter.

The brain's need for dopamine becomes so strong that it becomes consumed with the compulsion to feel euphoric once again. I feel like a vampire in a room full of blood donors. It's a horrible feeling, and I never want to feel that way again.

I've also been able to spend a bit more time with Erika. She's beautiful, but she's also quite bright.

Two nights ago, we held a meeting, and Seth said something she disagreed with. He said that if God were here today, he'd destroy all the drugs and alcohol in the world to save people from their addictions.

Erika disagreed, saying that she believes the world works from the *outside* in, but God works from the *inside* out.

She said the world's solution would be to take people out of the slums, but God's solution is to take the slums out of people, who then take themselves out of the slums. She said that the world tries to change our environment, but God changes our hearts, and then we change our environment.[3]

I'm not sure I understand what she said, but it was a compelling statement. I thought about it for a long time that night—which surprised me. I've decided she was saying that God changes men, and changed men change the world. I think I saw that on a Facebook post one time.

---

[3] Ezra Taft Benson, Conference Report, October 1985, pp. 5-6.

The whole "God" thing is hard for me—not so much whether God exists or not—but that He cares enough about me to help me with my personal issues. I mean, if God is everyone's God, how does He have time for me? Especially when there are so many better—and worse—people than me in the world.

I've struggled with the "Higher Power" thing because I felt like God abandoned me when Nate died. For the longest time, I couldn't understand—if God is so kind and loving—why'd he let that happen? I decided that if He wasn't powerful enough to save Nate, He's not powerful enough to help me stop using drugs.

It's funny because my very first sponsor told me that I could make anything my Higher Power, even a tree or a doorknob. So I tried making a tree my Higher Power, but I eventually decided that a tree has no more power to save than belief in an imaginary being who supposedly loves us so much that He died for us. It just hasn't worked for me, but then again, neither has the tree.

Erika did make a good point, though. I've tried to change my environment a dozen times, but I always end up going back to drugs. I've tried moving to different places, changing lifestyles, making new friends—none of it has worked. If there were a way to change my heart, maybe it would matter less what my environment is and matter more about what I become.

I've talked to Drew quite a bit since I got here, and he's helping me look at recovery differently than I ever did before. If it weren't for him, I'd still be searching for that mystical tree that I wanted to make my higher power.

Drew is from Salt Lake City, and he's a Mormon. I didn't know much about Mormons before I met him, but a couple of people in my school went to that church. Unfortunately, I didn't know any of them that well. So, now having met Drew, I wish I did.

The only thing I knew about Mormons was that they didn't believe in birth control, and they'd knock on your door at the most inopportune moments. Since ours is a private, gated neighborhood that doesn't allow soliciting of any kind, they never knocked on our door, but I did meet them once.

One afternoon in high school, I was at a girl's house after school. We weren't dating or anything, but we sat next to one another in biology class and became study partners. That's probably when I first recognized divine grace because she was the cutest girl in the class.

We were supposed to be studying, but I couldn't keep my eyes off her. So what started as a little flirting eventually led to kissing and, well, you know where kissing leads.

I guess I was moving a little too quickly because when my hands started roaming, she got very nervous and said she had to go to the bathroom. When she returned, I wanted to pick up where we left off, but just as we started kissing again, the doorbell rang.

I mean, the timing could not have been any worse. She jumped up, ran to the door to see who it was, and came back with a couple of guys in white shirts and ties. They looked about the same age as us, maybe a little older, but they introduced themselves as missionaries for the Mormon church.

They asked if I'd like to hear a message about Jesus Christ. Apparently, this girl was also a Mormon, and the missionaries said they felt like they needed to drop by and see her at that exact moment. I had no desire to hear them preach, so I made an excuse that I had something else to do and left.

Anyway, back to Drew, he's been helping me understand that it's possible to have a personal relationship with God. I've always had this notion that God was some all-seeing, all-knowing, universal puppet-master who controls everything that happens in our lives. I always thought that God allows good and bad things to happen to us, depending on His mood. If we are good and follow the commandments, He's happy with us. If we do bad things, He gets angry, and our reward is whatever cruel punishment pleases Him most.

Drew explained things differently to me. He says that God is our Father in Heaven, the father of our spirits, which reside in our earthly bodies, and that we are His children. He says that God loves us regardless of what we do, or don't do, in our lives. He blesses us more when we follow His commandments, but He doesn't cause bad things to happen when we don't.

Drew also gave me a book that I've watched him read almost every day but never got the courage to ask him about it. It's called The Book of the Mormons, or something like that. I haven't read it much yet, but I promised him I would.

When Drew gave me the book, he shared a couple of passages that helped him understand why we go through difficult times in life. Drew knows about Nate and why I've had such a hard time trusting God.

One passage said that God gives us weaknesses so that we become humble. It said that when we're humble, we're teachable, and when we're teachable, we're changeable. Understanding that has helped me understand what Erika said about God changing our hearts. Once our hearts are in the right place, we have the power to change ourselves and then the things around us.

* * * * *

The German Shepard is sleeping and doesn't open his eyes until the truck comes to a stop. We park on a small mesa overlooking an area of high plains, but there is not one cow in sight.

"What are we looking for again?" I ask as we get out of the truck.

"Folks moved a herd of cattle through here earlier. Said there's a cow that might be stuck in a mire."

"What's a mire?"

"It's something cows get stuck in, Jake." Pit Bull snaps.

It surprises me that cattle would be in this area or that any of it could be wet enough for a cow to get stuck. All I see from the mesa are sagebrush and scrub pines.

"You go down around that side, and I'll check this side," he says, "Make sure you look around them trees. If a cow gets hot, she'll lie down in the shade of a tree. Holler if you find the cow. If not, I'll meet you back here in 15 minutes."

He puts the tailgate down and calls for the dog as I start walking down an embankment in the direction he told me to go. Unfortunately, I'm not wearing a watch, so I'll just have to guess when it feels like 15 minutes have passed.

A few minutes later, a noise behind me almost scares me out of my underwear. As I spin around, I expect a cougar to leap onto me from the top of a big rock, but it's just the German Shepard, and he's just strolling along behind me.

"Holy crap! I scream as my heart rate maxes out at 180. "You scared the heck out of me."

The dog doesn't seem to care and sits down at my feet, waiting for me to move on. I want to pet him, but I'm still too timid around dogs to know when it's safe to do so. He doesn't look threatening, but then I'm no dog whisperer.

Together, we search around for every tree within a quarter-mile of the mesa and then decide it's time to head back. There's no sign of a cow up here, but I see some great hiding places for rattlesnakes. My nerves are already on edge because it just feels like I'm going to step on one any second.

As I climb onto the mesa where the truck is parked, Pit Bull sits on the tailgate like he's been there the whole time I've been out searching.

"Any luck?" I ask.

"Nope," he replies, swinging his feet and resting on the palms of his hands. "But it looks like you're making all kinds of new friends, aren't ya, Jake?"

The German Shepard walks past me and sniffs Pit Bull's boots before lying down in the shade of the truck.

"Yeah, I guess so," I say. "He's a beautiful dog. What's his name?"

"Judas," Pit Bull says as he hops down from the tailgate and looks at the dog at his feet.

"Seriously?" I ask as I climb up into the back of the truck, using a back tire as a step. "Why do you call him that?"

"Because he's a traitor," Pit Bulls says as he draws his pistol and shoots the dog in the head.

"*What the hell?*" I scream with the sound of the gunshot still in my ears.

"A dog that don't obey is no use to me, Jake. I told him to follow me, and he didn't."

He picks the dead dog up and lifts him over the tailgate, setting him down next to me in the bed of the truck. "That's just how things are around here," he says as he opens the driver's-side door. "I tell you to do something, and you don't do it…there's gonna be consequences."

My emotions are all over the place on the ride back down the mountain. I'm angry, I'm scared, but I'm mostly just sad. I don't understand what just happened. How could someone just shoot a dog like that, especially his *own* dog?

When we get back to the alfalfa field, the guys are finished, and so am I. As soon as I get back to the cabin, I will pack my bags and leave. If Pit Bull doesn't kill me, I'm likely to kill him, so whether I stay or go, I figure it pretty much ends the same way.

* * * * *

"Think about it for a minute," Drew says. "If you leave, they'll lock you away for a year. Is that what you want?"

"Of course not! I want that bastard to pay for what he did."

"How is that going to help you, Jake? If you leave here, you're going to jail, right? If you do something to Pit Bull, he's either going to kill you, or you're going to jail. Which of those outcomes sound good to you?"

"Yeah, but either way, I'm getting out of here."

"And then what? Think this through, all the way to the end. If you do anything, you lose everything."

"So, what do you want me to do?" I yell, throwing my hands in the air.

"Let it go."

I nearly punch Drew in the face when he says that, but I don't. Instead, I just sit down on the edge of Todd's bunk and rub dirt off my face.

"I need to talk to The Warden. She needs to know what's going on."

"What? Do you think *she's* going to be sympathetic about a dog that got shot here on the ranch? You met her. She doesn't care what happens to a dog. As long as we keep working, the ranch keeps going. That's all she cares about."

"I'll go talk to Dr. Hartwell, then. He's the one who turned this place into a place for addicts, right? So I'll tell him what's going on."

"Good luck with that," Seth interjects, "He's so sick he can't even get out of bed."

"What's he like?" I ask.

"Don't know," Seth replies, "I've never met him."

"What do you mean you haven't met him? Has anyone met him?"

Seth thinks about it a minute and then turns to Drew. "Drew, you ever met Dr. Hartwell?"

"No, they said they found out he has cancer right before I got here. I've seen a doctor, or a nurse, come and go, but I've never met him."

"Look," Drew reasons, "He's pretty much out of the picture, and Sue has enough on her plate with this ranch and cows mysteriously disappearing."

"I hear the bank is about to take over the ranch too," Seth adds.

"Where'd you hear that?" Drew asks.

"From Monica. She's friends with that dude from Wenatchee—you know, the male nurse who does the intakes here?"

"What did he tell Monica?"

"He said that unless they get more patients coming in here paying for treatment, the bank is going to foreclose on the loan and put this place up for auction. Apparently, the bank is just waiting for Dr. Hartman to die before they call in the note. They don't want to be the reason he suddenly croaks—wouldn't be good for business, you know?"

"How did he know that?"

"He said they've laid off a bunch of staff and cut his hours way back. The Warden's even working the reception desk when new patients arrive."

"Seriously?" Drew asks.

"She's the first person I met when I got here," I confirm. "Oh, wait, that's not true—Vanessa was the first person I met. Why doesn't she help out if things are so bad?"

"She doesn't get along with The Warden," Seth replies. "She's Sue's step-daughter, and neither of them wants the other to get any money from the sale of the ranch."

"I thought you said that if they sold the ranch, the bank would get the money to pay off the loan."

"The bank would get *some* of the money—sure, enough money to pay off the loan—but just look at this place. The land alone will bring in a ton of cash. Add to that the cattle? The lodge? These cabins? Vanessa stands to inherit all of it."

"I don't get it. If there are money problems, why don't they just sell some of the property?"

"Sue doesn't want to," Seth explains. "This land's been in her family for generations. She wants to hold onto it…every last acre of it. She doesn't want to see Vanessa get *anything*, and Vanessa's the only one left to inherit this place when The Doc and The Warden are gone. I don't know what the loan conditions are, but it sounds like if the bank calls in the note, they have to liquidate all assets, including the ranch, to make sure the debts are paid. If that happens, the Warden and Vanessa split the cash because both the ranch and the loan are in Dr. Hartwell's name."

I stop pacing for a minute when I realize that Terd has been quiet for a while. He didn't take it well when I told him what happened to the German Shepard.

"You alright, Todd?"

"Yeah," he says, but he's lying on his bunk facing the wall, and I think he's been crying.

"Hey, what was his *real* name?" I ask as I sit down on the end of his bed. "I know it wasn't Judas."

"Shasta."

"Well, Shasta's in a better place now, right?"

"I guess so," Terd says. "He was a good dog. He didn't deserve to die that way."

"You're right," Drew says. "He didn't deserve that, but like Jake said, He *is* in a better place now."

"Do you think God cares what happens to a dog?" Terd asks.

If it were anyone else, I'd question the sincerity of the question, but I can tell Todd is taking this hard.

"I know He does," Drew explains, sitting across the room on his own bunk.

"The bible says that not even a sparrow falls to the ground without God knowing it. We had this little dog once." Drew continues. "He was one of those Weiner dogs, you know—long body and really short legs?"

"His name was Kennedy, and he was an awesome dog. We taught him to shake, sit up, roll over, all kinds of things. But the most incredible thing he could do was catch a frisbee in his mouth."

"My family has always had this one night each week that we spend together—Monday night. We call it Family Home Evening. Well, one night, we were playing a game of horseshoes in the backyard."

"My brother threw a horseshoe, and just as it was about to land, Kennedy jumped for it like it was a frisbee, and it hit him in the head. He dropped like a sack of potatoes. We ran to him, but he wasn't breathing—honest to God, he was dead."

"Oh, that's a *great* story," Seth says. "Does anyone else have a sadder story than that he can tell to make Terd feel better?"

"Shut up, Seth," Drew says, "I'm not finished yet. So, my mom is freaking out, right? My little brother is crying, and my dad is looking at this dog, trying to figure out what to do. All I could think of doing was to say a prayer."

"A prayer?" I ask. "You, like, knelt down and said a prayer?"

"I did," Drew confirmed. "I dropped to my knees and said, 'Heavenly Father, I love this dog, please don't let him die.'"

"Do you know what happened next? My dad picked Kennedy up, cradled him in his arms, and put his mouth over the dog's mouth and nose. He gave him two breaths, a couple of chest compressions, and guess what? Kennedy's eyes opened, and he started breathing again."

"No way!" Seth says, "Did that really happen?"

"True story, I swear," Drew says, "My dad gave a dog CPR and saved his life!"

Terd is smiling again.

"My point is, Todd, that God does care what happens to a dog. And if He cares that much about a dog, then why wouldn't He feel the same about you or me? Why wouldn't He help any of us?"

The room is entirely silent for the next few minutes. It gives me a chance to think about what Drew just said and let it sink in. What he said actually makes sense.

"So, what do we have to do for God to help us?" I ask.

"We just have to *believe*."

"Believe what?" I ask, recalling the words from Step 2 that I've recited hundreds of times. "That He can restore us to sanity?"

"No." Drew explains. "Not just that God *can* restore us to sanity, but that He *will*."

* * * * *

When the evening chores are done, I walk down to the lake, alone, with only my thoughts as company. It's peaceful here in the evening, with the lake reflecting the sun as it drops below the horizon. I've started coming out here more and more often to reflect on things, and tonight I have a great deal on my mind.

When Nate died, I was angry. I was mad at myself for not being able to save him. I was mad at my father for not keeping a better eye on him, and I was angry at God for letting him die.

Because of what happened, I decided I must not be important to God. I told myself that I wasn't good enough for God to love me. Why else would He let Nate die?

It wasn't difficult to convince myself that He only loves people who go to church every Sunday, and put their offerings in the plate, and forgive those who hurt them. It was just easier to believe that than come up with a better explanation for why I was so sad and angry.

Tonight, however, I find myself asking questions I've never considered. If God really does care what happens to a sparrow or a dog, why wouldn't He help Drew, me, or any of us?

Even though I don't know Drew all that well, I know he is sincere in his belief in God. I've watched him closely since I arrived, and there is something different about him. He doesn't just profess to believe in God—he *really* does. There is a conviction about him. I think if there is anyone here who has a chance at staying clean, it's him.

The first night I spent here at the ranch, I heard someone get out of bed after the lights went out. At first, I thought Seth was getting down from his bunk to use the bathroom, but it was Drew.

When my eyes adjusted to the dark, I saw Drew kneeling at the side of his bed. He didn't say anything out loud, but I knew he was praying. I've also seen him praying in the morning, just before the power comes back on in the cabins.

I'm not usually one to talk about religion. If someone wants to believe in God, that's fine, so long as they don't try to push their beliefs on me. When the topic of God, a Higher Power, or spirituality comes up, I'm usually racing every other agnostic to the door. However, I don't feel that way when Drew talks about God.

Something Drew said tonight keeps echoing in my head. He said that it's not enough just believing in God or believing He has the power to help me. Drew said I have to believe that He *will* help me.

I've never had that kind of faith in God. But, since nothing else has worked, maybe it's time I try.

CHAPTER 7

Over the past couple of weeks, I've noticed that the sun rises over the mountains to the east a minute or two earlier each morning, and it sets a minute or two later each evening. Maybe that's why it feels like some days are longer than others—like my first day on a horse.

"C'mon, Jake," Erika says as she leads the horse from his stall to the corral behind the lodge. "Riding a horse isn't hard."

I've never ridden a horse before, so my heart is thumping in my chest. I feel like I'm about to get on a roller coaster, and I get motion sickness in elevators.

It dawns on me as we walk toward the corrals that I've never actually stood next to a horse. I've seen horses grazing in pastures next to the road and parades, but I've never stood next to one and looked in the eye.

The first thing I notice is how tall and muscular this horse is. Anytime he moves, his muscles flex like there's something alive crawling under his skin. His physique is simply astonishing, his coat a reddish-brown that reminds me of Shasta's eyes.

I'm a little over six feet tall, and I can barely see over this horse at its shoulders. I don't think he's as big as the Budweiser Clydesdales, but I just hope he's not too much horse for me.

The second thing I notice is that horses have a smell. I wouldn't call it an odor because it's not like walking into a high school locker room after football practice. It's more of a scent—a combination of dirt, sweat, and leather. It's an earthy scent—kind of like a forest.

My great grandfather on my father's side lived in Idaho when I was a kid. He had this underground root cellar in a barn where they stored potatoes, carrots, and other root vegetables after the harvest. Regardless of the temperature outside, the cellar maintained a constant temperature between 32- and 40-degrees Fahrenheit year-round.

I remember the smell when he'd open the hatch and let us climb down the ladder. It was more of a pit than a room, and it had a wood ceiling and a dirt floor. Grandpa Jensen had to duck a little to get around in there, but for us kids, it was like being in a hobbit hole. I wanted to camp out down there until my grandpa told me about the worms that come out at night. Of course, he might have just been teasing me, but I wasn't going to find out.

I still remember the smell of the root cellar because the horse's scent is the closest thing I've ever smelt to it. So I don't care what his hame is. I'm calling him "Jensen."

Erika has obviously been around horses before because she's pretty comfortable with the blanket, saddle, and the thing that fits in the horses' mouth. I think she called a bit, but a bit of what? I have no idea. When I see the size of this horses' teeth, I put my hands in my pockets so that he doesn't think my fingers are carrots.

"Okay," Erika says, with the horses' reins in her left hand. "Anytime you mount a horse, you want to do it from his left side because that's what he'll be expecting. If you approach from the other side, you'll frighten him."

"The most important thing to remember is that he takes his cues from you. So, if you want him to be calm, you have to be calm. If you're nervous, he'll be nervous. And if you're scared, he'll be scared.

Erika shows me how to put my boot in the stirrup and swing my right leg over the horse. In one swift motion, she's off the ground and into the saddle.

Just to be fair, she makes it look a lot easier than it really is. As soon as I put my foot in the stirrup, the horse starts to shimmy away from me. I put one foot back on the ground to regain my balance, but my other boot is stuck in the stirrup, and I end up dancing the two-step with a horse I just met.

Erika uses the reigns to stop the horse and rubs him on the nose. "Settle," she says in a calm voice, using what must be horse psychology. Just like that, she has him back under control.

"You have to relax, Jake, and move a bit slower. You want the horse to trust you, not be afraid of you."

"Okay, let me try it again," I say, using the saddle horn to help me balance this time.

I follow Erika's advice and avoid any sudden movements the horse won't expect. This time I'm much smoother as I try to get in the saddle, and I'm rewarded with a horse that stands perfectly still.

"That's it," Erika says, "now just ease into the saddle and keep your legs relaxed. See, that wasn't so hard, was it?"

"No, but you still have hold of the reins. What's he going to do once I take them?"

"Whatever you tell him to do."

"You mean I talk to him? Like, tell him when to turn left or turn right?"

She laughs. "No, Jake. If you want a horse to halt, first, lean back in the saddle and shift your weight toward the back of the horse. You also want to have the stirrups under the balls of your feet. Push them forward like you're putting on the brakes in a car. Then, you want to pull slightly on the reins, keeping them low near the saddle horn. That's how you talk to a horse."

Erika hands me the reins, and I tighten up, thinking that the horse will bolt any second. As a result, he senses my nervousness and starts to dance.

"Relax, Jake," Erika says again. "Whatever you're feeling, he's feeling. So just relax, but sit up straight while I adjust the stirrups.

I'm even more nervous than I was before, but I force myself to relax. My legs comply but not my upper body—I still hold the reins like I would a winning lottery ticket.

Erika adjusts the stirrups so that they are the correct length for my legs and asks, "Okay, are you ready to go for a ride?"

I have no idea if I'm ready or not, but it doesn't matter. Erika makes a "clicking" sound with her mouth, and the horse starts to walk forward. The sudden movement surprises me, and I instinctively pull on the reins to make the horse stop.

"Relax, Jake," Erika coaches just above a whisper. "Give him the reins—let him lead. He's not going to do anything crazy or dangerous."

"Give *him* the reins?" I ask, looking at the leather straps she just gave me. "I thought I was supposed to hold on to these."

"It means to give him some *slack* in the reins. Give him some freedom to walk around."

"But what if I don't want him free to walk around? What happens if I give him some slack and he just starts running?"

"He won't, Jake, but if you're holding the reigns tight, trying to control his every move, you'll never get anywhere. Give him some reins and squeeze him gently with your legs."

The horse moves forward gently when I do this, and we make a few clockwise circles around the corral. After a few more passes, I realize the horse won't run wild unless he gets spooked.

I'm also learning that riding a horse is not the same as driving a car—at least not the steering part. For example, I thought that if I wanted the horse to walk around the corral in a left-hand circle, I had to keep constant left input in the reins, but that's not true. The horse knows to walk in a circle because that's all he can do.

"Okay," Erika says, as she stands in the middle of the corral, "I want you to pull the left rein a bit more and get him to turn around and walk the other way."

To my surprise, the horse does what I want him to do, and I don't even have to pull on the right rein to straighten out and walk counterclockwise. He pretty much knows what to do without any input at all. It's just when I need to speed up or slow down, I give him a little squeeze or pull gently on the reins.

Once Erika feels I've got the hang of it, she leads her horse out of his stall and mounts him just outside the corral. To my amazement, and without a word or input to the reins, she gets the horse to walk forward, stop, and then back up so that she can open the gate of the corral without getting off the horse.

"Ready to go for a little ride?" she asks.

"I think so," I reply, with as much confidence as I can muster. "Where are we going?"

"Let's just walk the horses along that trail that goes around the lake," she says. That should give us a good 20 minutes to make sure you're ready to go out in the open. After that, we'll head down the road and meet up with the others."

The rest of the afternoon went far better than I anticipated. The ride around the lake is beautiful, and both the horse and I get comfortable with one another. I don't know about the horse, but if you ask me, we even start to feel like we're a team.

Once we finish, we ride up the road and through a couple of fields to join the other inmates and prison guards. The weather is supposed to get nasty for the next couple of days, and they've been out here rounding up the cattle and bringing them closer to the corrals.

"Check it out," Terd says when he sees Erika and me approach. "Jake's ridin' a horse!"

"What?" I reply. "You didn't think I could?"

"We took bets on whether or not you'd be able to get the horse out of the corral," Seth says, "Now I owe Terd *ten* bucks."

"Thanks! It's just like ridin' a bike but bumpier. Do they not make cushions for these saddles?"

I ride between Terd and another inmate for the rest of the afternoon as we drive the herd back toward the lodge. After that, it will be easier for us to check on them, feed them, and they'll be less likely to get in trouble during the storm.

SERENITY RANCH

Terd explains the organization for herding cattle as we ride. Because we have a good-sized herd of over 600 cattle, we have a crew of 8 people—3 experienced prison guards and 5 inmates.

The trail boss rides in the point position, in front of, or near the front, of the herd. That gives the cows something to follow. He also controls the speed at which the herd moves. The trail boss must know the terrain, the animals, and where they are going.

Behind the trail boss rides two riders in the swing position, one on each side of the herd about a third of the way back. The swingers' job is to keep the herd together and watch out for any cows that may try to break away. They help steer the cattle when the herd turns, and they also back up the trail boss if, for any reason, he leaves the point position.

Next, come the flankers. They're positioned about two-thirds of the way back, and their job is to back up the swingers and keep the cattle bunched together. If they are not doing their job, the herd will fan out along the trail and become more difficult to herd.

Finally, at the rear are three horsemen riding drag. Even with a herd this size, you could probably do it with less than three, but I have no clue what I'm doing, and Terd can sometimes get distracted.

It's not his job, or any of the riders' job for that matter, to count cattle during the drive, but that's what Terd does. He is constantly zigzagging from side to side and standing up in his stirrups to get a better view.

All I can figure is that Terd must have an obsessive-compulsive disorder. He is obsessed with keeping track of how many cows are in the herd. Thankfully, a prison guard is riding with us who keeps the two of us in check.

By the time we get to the watering hole mid-way through the drive, I've already figured out why the newest guy is riding drag. You wouldn't think that Washington State is a desert with all the rain that falls in Seattle, but over here on the east side, the ground is dry and covered with rock and dust.

Even at the slow, meandering pace in which the herd is moving, the dust cloud that trails behind us must extend all the way to Idaho.

Terd, and the prison guard riding near me, have bandanas covering their faces. I have nothing except the neck of my t-shirt to protect my eyes, nose, and mouth from the irrepressible dust cloud that threatens to blind and suffocate me.

I don't know what Terd or this prison guard did to deserve the flank position, but I'm sure that my positioning has less to do with my experience driving cattle and more to do with my ongoing feud with Pit Bull. So you can guess who is riding point.

After five hours in the saddle, I couldn't be more thrilled to get down from the horse. I hear the dinner bell ring, but I'm skipping dinner and heading straight for the shower. I don't have much of an appetite tonight—I've been eating dust all afternoon.

*****

When we get back to the cabin after dinner and evening chores, Terd asks if we can start the meeting early. I'm not thrilled about sitting through a meeting tonight, but Terd has been really quiet lately, and maybe this will help with whatever is on his mind.

It's Seth's turn to lead the meeting, so when everyone gets there, he opens the meeting using an A.A. meeting format.

"Good evening. This is the regular meeting of the Serenity Ranch group of Alcoholics Anonymous. My name is Seth, and I am an addict."

"Alcoholics Anonymous is a fellowship of men and women who share their experience, strength, and hope with each other that they may solve their common problem and help others to recover from alcoholism. The only requirement for membership is a desire to stop drinking."

"There are no dues or fees for A.A. membership," Seth continues. "We are self-supporting through our own contributions. A.A. is not allied with any sect, denomination, politics, organization, or institution; does not wish to engage in any controversy; neither endorses nor opposes any causes. Our primary purpose is to stay sober and help other alcoholics to achieve sobriety."

"Jake will now read "How it Works" from Chapter 5 of the Big Book."

I have a laminated card Seth handed to me earlier, but I've heard this part enough times that I have it memorized. So I leave the card lying face down in front of me.

> Rarely have we seen a person fail who has thoroughly followed our path. Those who do not recover are people who cannot, or will not, completely give themselves to this simple program, usually men and women who are constitutionally incapable of being honest with themselves. There are such unfortunates. They are not at fault; they seem to have been born that way. They are naturally incapable of grasping and developing a manner of living which demands rigorous honesty. Their chances are less than average. There are those, too, who suffer from grave emotional and mental disorders, but many of them do recover if they have the capacity to be honest.
>
> Our stories disclose in a general way what we used to be like, what happened, and what we are like now. If you have decided that you want what we have and are willing to go to any length to get it—then you are ready to take certain steps.
>
> At some of these, we balked. We thought we could find an easier, softer way. But we could not. With all the earnestness at our command, we beg of you to be fearless and thorough from the very start. Some of us have tried to hold on to our old ideas, and the result was nil until we let go absolutely.
>
> Remember that we deal with alcohol—cunning, baffling, powerful! Without help, it is too much for us.

But there is One who has all power—that One is God. May you find Him now!

Half measures availed us nothing. We stood at the turning point. We asked His protection and care with complete abandon.

Here are the steps we took, which are suggested as a program of recovery.

The 12 steps in A.A. are almost identical to the 12 steps in N.A. The only difference is that rather than using the terms "drugs" and "addicts," A.A. uses the words "alcohol" and "alcoholics." An alcoholic or addict will find companionship in either organizaton that can help them achieve sobriety. Anyone with a desire to stop drinking or using drugs is welcome and will find peace and support with the same framework, traditions and principles regardless where in the world they meet.

Step 1: We admitted we were powerless over alcohol—that our lives had become unmanageable.

Step 2: Came to believe that a Power greater than ourselves could restore us to sanity.

Step 3: Made a decision to turn our will and our lives over to the care of God *as we understood Him.*

Step 4: Made a searching and fearless moral inventory of ourselves.

Step 5: Admitted to God, to ourselves, and to another human being the exact nature of our wrongs.

Step 6: Were entirely ready to have God remove all these defects of character.

Step 7: Humbly asked Him to remove our shortcomings.

Step 8: Made a list of all persons we had harmed, and became willing to make amends to them all.

Step 9: Made direct amends to such people wherever possible, except when to do so would injure them or others.

Step 10: Continued to take personal inventory and when we were wrong promptly admitted it.

Step 11: Sought through prayer and meditation to improve our conscious contact with God, *as we understood Him*, praying only for knowledge of His will for us and the power to carry that out.

Step 12: Having had a spiritual awakening as the result of these Steps, we tried to carry this message to alcoholics, and to practice these principles in all our affairs.

Many of us exclaimed, "What an order? I can't go through with it." Do not be discouraged. No one among us has been able to maintain anything like perfect adherence to these principles. We are not saints. The point is that we are willing to grow along spiritual lines. The principles we have set down are guides to progress. We claim spiritual progress rather than spiritual perfection."

"Our description of the alcoholic, the chapter to the agnostic, and our personal adventures before and after make clear three pertinent ideas: (a) That we were alcoholic and could not manage our own lives. (b) That probably no human power could have relieved our alcoholism. (c) That God could, and would if He were sought."[4]

"Thank you, Jake," Seth says. "This meeting is now open. Terd, did you want to go first?"

Terd is on the verge of tears before he even begins. "Something's been bothering me lately, and I need to get it off my chest. Maybe then I'll be able to sleep again. These past few nights, I haven't slept at all."

"Who are you, again?" Seth asks jokingly.

"Oh, sorry. My name is Todd, and I'm an addict. Some of you might already know that I'm a little awkward." A few people glance around the room, feigning a look of surprise. "I know it," Terd continues, "it's just how I've always been. I was diagnosed with ADHD and put on Ritalin, then Dexedrine, and later Adderall. But, unfortunately, all the medications did was make me feel worse."

"When I was in school, I got picked on a lot. Not just teased because I shouted out the answer to any question the teacher asked, but tormented day and night. I didn't have a single friend, and things got so bad that I thought about killing myself."

"There are only seven of us at this meeting, but it's the quietest I've ever heard it on the ranch. Even the rain outside falls without making a sound."

"About the time I turned fourteen, I got invited to a sleepover with some guys from school. I'd never been to a sleepover before, so I was really excited but also a little nervous. Most of the guys played on the football team, and I didn't want to say something stupid and have them laugh at me."

"When my dad dropped me off at the house where we would spend the night, you'd have thought my dad was the one going

---

[4] *Alcoholics Anonymous: The Story of How Many Thousands of Men and Women Have Recovered from Alcoholism,* (New York City, Alcoholics Anonymous World Services Inc., Fourth Edition, 2001) pp. 58-60.

instead of me. He was so excited that I finally had some friends that wanted to hang out with me. He said, 'Todd, you're a great kid. Just relax and have fun tonight." I remember turning around in the driveway to say something to him, but he was already on the phone with my mom, telling her how proud he was of me."

"That night, we watched a movie and played some games. There were girls and boys, but only the boys were staying over. The last game we played was kind of like 'Truth or Dare.' We sat in a circle, and when it was your turn, you had a choice, you could draw a 'truth' card or a 'dare' card, but you had to do what the card said."

"One of the 'truth' cards said something like, 'what's the most embarrassing thing that's ever happened to you?' Another said, 'what's the worst thing you've ever been caught doing?'

The 'dare' questions were more fun. For example, one girl had to unlock her cell phone and let everyone go through it for 5 minutes. She had some pictures she'd forgotten about and hadn't deleted. One of the guys had to kiss the girl in the circle that he knew the longest for 30 seconds—and it couldn't be his girlfriend either."

"When my turn came around, I picked a 'dare' card because I was afraid of what I might be asked to tell. My most embarrassing story was a lot worse than anyone knew. The card I drew said that I had to take the first person of the opposite sex to my right into a room and do whatever she told me to do."

"I was scared to death, but I had to go through with it. The girl to my right was Kristen Halverson. She was a cheerleader, like most of the girls there, and the prettiest girl in school. I'd always had a crush on her."

"We went into a bedroom and shut the door. Kristen asked me if I wanted to see her naked. I'd never seen a naked girl, so I said 'yes.' She said that she would undress if I undressed at the same time, but that I had to turn around and stare at the wall while she undressed."

"I took off my shirt and pants, but I was afraid to take off my underwear. Kristen told me that she was undressed and needed to take off my underwear or I couldn't see her. So, I took off my underwear and stood there until she said, 'Okay, you can turn around now.'"

"What I didn't know was that while I was undressing, Kristen had opened the door and let everyone else into the room. So, when I turned around, completely naked, everyone at the party was staring at me and taking pictures with their cell phones. Then, they all started laughing, even Kristen, because she was still completely dressed."

"I wanted to cry, but all I could do was grab my clothes and run out the back door. I got dressed behind a bush and went to the door to go back in. I was embarrassed, but I still wanted to have friends. But they'd locked the door. When I knocked, I could hear them laughing inside."

"The worst part was that I had to call my dad to get a ride home," Terd explained, as tears streamed down his face, "and I had to tell him what had happened."

"I'd never seen my dad cry before that night. It crushed him to see how the other kids treated me, and it nearly destroyed both of us. That's about the time I started doing drugs."

Erika gets up, walks over to Todd, and puts both arms around him. Monica is the next to do the same. Pretty soon, we're all in a giant bear hug with Todd in the middle.

"Todd," I say, "I'm so sorry that you went through all that, and I'm sorry if I've done anything to make you feel bad about yourself."

"Oh, no," Todd replies. "That's not what I have to get off my chest."

"What?" Seth asks. "That's not what's keeping you up at night?"

"No," Todd says. "It's what I did the next year to get back at those guys. I've never told anyone that I spiked their cooler of Gatorade with an entire bottle of an extra-strength laxative before the homecoming game."

"By the fourth quarter, seven players had shit themselves out on the field, and three cheerleaders had major blowouts during the halftime show. The best part was that I'd stolen all the rolls of toilet paper in the locker rooms and glued the toilets seats shut with instant epoxy."

"I've been feeling kind of bad about it lately and, since I hadn't told anyone about it, even during my Step 5, I thought it would be good to get it off my chest. Thanks for listening. I feel much better!"

When no one else speaks up, I decide it's time to share something that's been on my mind today. It's not as personal as Todd's story, but it's something I'd like the group to know.

"My name is Jake, and I'm an addict. I think most of you know that I haven't been around horses much before coming to the ranch. In fact, today, I realized that I've really never been around them at all."

"This morning, I had a chance to get on a horse for the first time. Erika volunteered to stay back and help me when the rest headed out to move the herd. I'm glad she did," I say, catching a smile come to her face when I glance at her sitting next to me.

"Erika kept repeating something to me today. She said I needed to let go and allow the horse to lead if I wanted to get somewhere. She explained that if I try to maintain too much control of the horse, he'll freeze up, and we won't get anywhere.

"It's interesting because that's the opposite of what I thought I needed to do. I thought I had to keep a tight hold on the reins, or the horse would just start running wild. But when I finally gave the horse some slack in the reins, he didn't go crazy. Instead, he just started walking forward, in the direction he knew we needed to go."

"I guess what struck me," I explain, "is that 'letting go' is possibly one of the biggest challenges I've had in changing my life. I have a hard time forgiving, forgetting, and allowing someone else to be in control. My mindset has always been, 'if you want something done right, you have to do it yourself. I always think I have the solution figured out—even though my plans always fall through."

"If you've been in recovery circles very long, you've probably heard people say, you have to '*let go*, and *let God*.' I think that's what Step 3 is about. Step 3 says, 'we made the decision to turn our *will* and our *lives* over to God.' I just didn't know how to do that until today."

"Believe me when I say that I've tried every other possible way to get clean, but I have never surrendered my will over to God. I've never placed my trust in Him and allowed Him to be the driving influence in my life. I need to start living the life He wants me to live rather than the life I want to live. I just need to let go…and let God."

CHAPTER 8

I trust weathermen about as much as I trust rattlesnakes. Still, their predictions for a mighty storm rolling off the Pacific couldn't have been more accurate. Heavy wind and rain lashed the cabin throughout the night, and it's still raining hard when I awake.

To my surprise, however, it isn't the lights turning on in our cabin that wakes me; it's heavy pounding on the door by someone with a voice I don't recognize.

"Get up! Power's out. We ride out to check on the cows at first light."

Lightning strikes not far away and illuminates the inside of the cabin for a split second, but then we're back in the dark, scrambling for clothes, jeans, and something to keep us dry.

Because of the valley's location, the high mountains block the easterly flow of the storm and create a venturi effect through the valley, where the velocity of the wind increases exponentially. The result is gale-force winds ripping through the valley, downing power lines, and scaring every living creature—especially cows.

Drew and I ride out with another prison guard in the pouring rain. I'm not sure how safe it is for me to be on a horse, but I don't think my safety is as much a concern to Pit Bull as is the condition of the cows.

"Besides," Terd said, just before he and Seth headed off in another direction, "if you've got to ford a swollen stream, you're safer on a horse than in a vehicle."

Apparently, a horse has a higher clearance than trucks, which are more likely to get caught in the current and carried downstream. (Huh, I didn't know that—I just figured it was because horses can swim.)

We follow the road as far as we can, but we discover that a fallen tree knocked out the main power line to the ranch. The prison guard gets Pit Bull on the radio and tells him what we found and where. I halfway expect Pit Bull to send one of us up a ladder to make the repairs, but he relays back that The Warden is calling the power company.

Since the power line may be still "alive," we cut through a wooded section and reconnect with the main road a quarter mile down the mountain. I'm nervous about riding a horse in the rain, but I just let my horse follow the other two horses and hope everything turns out okay.

When we get to the pasture where the cows are, my first thought is one of complete disaster. There isn't a cow on its feet. Instead, every cow in sight is lying on the ground—some huddled together, others spread out.

I'm about to ask the prison guard if they're dead when Drew explains to me that cows take cover in a storm by lying down. Apparently, they are less likely to get struck by lightning. So if you ever see cows lie down in a field, it means there's a storm approaching.

"So, they aren't dead?" I ask.

"Nah. Scared, but not dead," Drew replies. "Still, we need to make sure none have broken through the fence and wandered off."

"Isn't there a cow tracking system they could get for these cows?" I ask, wiping the rain out of my eyes. "You know, RFID tags, or collars, or something?"

"Oh, yeah," Drew says. "I read an article about that in *Beef Magazine*."

"Are you serious?" I ask.

"Sure," Drew says excitedly. "There are some great GPS tracking systems too, that can tell you if a cow is sick, injured, in heat, or not eating enough. Sends the information right to your cell phone."

"No, I mean, is there really something called *Beef Magazine*?"

"Sure is!"

"And it has nothing to do with gay porn?"

Drew laughs, "Think about this, Jake. There are over 700,000 cattle ranches in the U.S. alone. And over 27% of all land is used for livestock grazing.[5] It's a huge business!"

He wipes the rain off his face and never stops smiling. "You know what the best part is?" He asks. "It's simple, blue-collar workers like you and me riding out in weather like this every day, making sure people have food on their table come dinnertime. It ain't some big shot corporate president living in a fancy penthouse in New Jersey getting' it done. This, right here, is what America is all about."

I don't bother telling Drew that my father owns a luxury penthouse in Midtown Manhattan or that he made his fortune by perfecting artificial pharmaceutical enhancements. Everyone has a different idea of the American dream, and I hope Drew gets to live his.

After checking on the cattle, the prison guard rides over and tells us there's another break in the fence and sends Drew back to get the fence-stretching tool and some wire. He takes me down to the broken section and tells me to stay there and make sure no cattle get out. He's going to get a headcount and make sure none of the cows are missing.

Standing in the pouring rain is miserable when you have nothing but a baseball hat and a nylon jacket. I thought I was wet an hour ago, but now I can feel rivulets of water flowing down my neck,

---

[5] https://www.neogen.com/neocenter/blog/fast-facts-state-of-u-s-cattle-ranching.

across the small of my back, and down the insides of my legs. The water in my boots is three inches deep and rising.

When your jacket, t-shirt, underwear, and jeans are so wet they stick to you like mine are right now, it feels like you jumped into a swimming pool. But, at least, underwater, your clothes don't add twenty pounds of dead weight.

When Drew gets back, there's a break in the rain, and he shows me how to mend the fence using the tool and the extra strands of barb wire he brought back. As we're stretching the broken wire, something catches his eye.

"Check this out," Drew says, pointing to the shiny edge on the end of the wire.

"What is it? All I see is rusty barb wire that the Warden should've replaced years ago."

"Look at the end," he says. "See that beveled edge and how shiny it is?"

"Yeah, so what?"

"This wire didn't break—it was cut."

"You mean on purpose?"

"Looks like it to me," Drew says. "Someone wanted these cows to escape."

"Why would anyone do that?"

"I don't know. Maybe that Goodman guy? He wants to buy this land, right? Maybe he's trying to rustle cattle out of here too."

Just then, the prison guard rides up and announces, "We're missin' a dozen head."

"See, this is why they need a tracking system," I say.

"What's he talkin' about?" The prison guard asks.

"Nothing," Drew says. "Those devices are thousands of dollars apiece, Jake. The Doc ain't never gonna spend that kind of money on these cows."

"I'm gonna call this in. We're gonna need some help findin' them cows," the prison guard says.

"Hold on a second," I say as I walk over to my horse. "Check this out."

Drew and the prison guard come over and peer down at the ground where I'm looking. "Tire tracks."

In rain like this, mud is everywhere, but we're looking at fresh tire tracks in the soil in a section of a field where vehicles don't usually drive.

"See how the tread left indentations in the mud and how the mud is pushed up here on the side of the tracks? These tracks are new—at least since the rain started."

"Maybe someone's been out here already and saw the broken fence," the prison guard says.

"Did anyone tell you there was a broken fence?" I ask.

"What? You think I'm stupid?" the prison guard asks. "I'd a brought the tools if I knew it was busted."

"Hey, come over here, you guys," Drew yells, calling us over to a section near the fence line. "See how there're only two sets of tire tracks back there, but there are four sets where they make this turn?"

"Yeah, so what?" the prison guard says, unable to see what Drew and I have already figured out.

"These tracks were made by a truck pulling a trailer," Drew explains. "Whoever it was, backed the trailer up to the opening in the fence here."

"Why would anyone do that?" the prison guard asks.

"Dude, how much meth did you smoke?" Drew asks. "We're not gonna find the missing cows out here. Someone loaded them up and hauled them away."

* * * * *

By the time we get back to the corral, it's raining again, even harder than it was before. The wind has picked up again, too, and sheets of rain force us into the horse corrals just to talk to one another.

"I'm gonna go tell Pit Bull what we found," the prison guard says. "He ain't gonna be happy about this."

"Tell him to check the security cameras," Drew says. "Maybe they got some video of a truck and trailer moving through here last night."

Drew and I rub the horses down and dry them the best we can before putting a blanket on them and leading them into their stalls. If you put horses away wet, they get chilled, especially in the wind—and chilled horses can get sick. We also give them some fresh water and feed.

I'm freezing when we get back to the cabin. Drew beats me to the bathroom, so I strip out of my clothes as fast as I can and dry myself off with a towel. I'm envisioning how great a hot shower is going to feel when Drew comes out of the bathroom wrapped in a towel and shivering more than me.

"No hot water," he says. "Power is still out."

"Great!" I mutter through chattering teeth. "Then I'm going back to bed."

"What about breakfast? Aren't you hungry?"

"Not enough to get dressed and go back out in that rain."

"Okay, well, I'm gonna see if they saved us anything. I'll bring you back a plate if there is."

As Drew gets dressed, I get enough courage to ask him something that's been on my mind for a while.

"Hey, Drew, can I ask you something before you go?"

"Sure. What's up?"

"The other night, you said that we must not only believe that God *can* heal us—we must believe that he *will*. How do I do that when I don't even know how to have faith in God?"

Drew turns around and sits on his bunk across from mine. "Faith is believing in something we can't see, but that we know is true," he begins. "For example, how do you know the sun will rise tomorrow?"

"I'm not sure it will with this storm out there."

"Okay," he says, laughing. "Aside from the weather, how do you know that light will displace the darkness tomorrow morning?"

"Because it always does. The sun rises every morning. It's a fact."

"Yes, it is," Drew confirms, "and because it always does, you have perfect faith that the sun will rise tomorrow, right?"

"Yes."

"Having faith in God is the same thing. The Bible says that Jesus Christ is the same yesterday, today, and tomorrow—in other words, He doesn't change.[6] If He changed, we wouldn't be able to trust Him. But because He does *not* change, we can have perfect faith that He will do exactly what He says He will do."

"You know the book I gave you the other day? There's a verse in there that says that having faith does not mean that we must have a perfect knowledge of things. In fact, faith is *not* a perfect knowledge, but rather a *hope* that what we believe is true."

"In that book, there is also a story—actually, it's more of a parable. Anyway, this man plants a seed, and he does so, believing that one day it will become something more than just a seed. However, instead of just walking away and hoping that the seed will do something, he takes a particular interest in it and looks after it. He waters it regularly. He makes sure the soil has the proper nutrients. And he is careful that it gets just the right amount of sunshine."

"After a little while, the seed begins to swell, and one day he sees a tiny green sprout coming out of the ground where he planted the seed. When the man sees this sprout, he knows the seed is growing, and he commits himself to helping the little sprout to flourish."

"After many years of cultivating the seed, watering it, measuring its growth, and believing that it will become something great, he is blessed with a full-grown tree that brings forth fruit that he can eat. This magnificent tree came out of a tiny seed that he planted with the hope that it would grow."

---

[6] Hebrews 13:8, *The Holy Bible*, King James Version.

"Believing in, trusting in, and having faith in God works the same way. In fact, God invites us to experiment and plant in our hearts our own seed of faith that His word is true. Planting a seed takes faith, not a lot, but just enough to act on our hope that it will grow into something bigger. In fact, God says, in the beginning, all we need to have is a 'particle of faith.' And if we nourish whatever faith we can muster--by feeding it, tending it, and caring for it, our little seed will, over time, grow into a strong and mighty tree of faith."

"So, for us, we start by planting a seed in our hearts that God lives and that He loves us. As we water that seed by praying, recognizing His goodness, and following His commandments—we begin to feel the seed growing in our hearts until it brings forth fruit."

"But what does that fruit look like?" I ask. "I want Him to fix my life, not give me something to eat."

"The fruit of this tree isn't *food*, Jake. It is the faith to act on God's word. It is having a perfect knowledge that God will do His part when he says, 'Ask, and ye shall receive; knock, and it shall be opened unto you.' It is having perfect faith that when we *do* ask, He will give to us that which we seek in righteousness."

"So, where does that leave me?" I ask. "How do I plant this seed?"

"You've already done it, Jake." You planted the seed when you stopped me from walking out that door and asked me how to have faith in God's word. You planted it when you had even just *a desire to believe* that what I said was true. Now all you have to do is nourish that seed and help it grow."

"And I do that by praying and by keeping His commandments?"

"Yes!" Drew says with a smile on his face. "And by believing that He will help you."

"How does this fit in with giving our will and our life over to God?"

"I'm glad you asked Jake because what I'm about to tell you will have a greater effect on your recovery than anything else I know. It is a truth that I have just recently begun to understand myself, and it is how you and I will free ourselves from our addictions."

"Okay. I'm ready. Let me hear it."

"God said, 'Behold, I stand at the door and knock; if any man hear my voice, and open the door, I will come in to him.'"

"You see," Drew continues, "God gave us our agency to choose, and not just between right and wrong, but also whether we want His help and influence in our lives. We have to open the door. He will not come into our house unless we invite Him."

"The most amazing aspect of giving our will over to God is that, even with all His power and glory, God will never *compel* us to obey Him. He will never force us to do something that we don't want to do. Instead, our Heavenly Father wants us to obey Him because of our love for Him—just as He loves you and me."

"Our Heavenly Father wants us to become *willing* to keep His commandments. Because when we become *willing* and turn our lives over to Him, He can help us become greater than we could ever be on our own."

* * * * * *

The storm's fury dissipates by dinnertime, but now it's just a steady rain that shows no sign of letting up. We spent most of the afternoon getting ready for the Warden to inspect our cabins. She said there was no excuse not to have our personal areas clean enough to eat off the floor with the downtime we have due to the storm.

Seth and Todd can't seem to keep their areas clean to save their lives. Neither of them has enough sense to put their dirty clothes in the suitcases under our bunks instead of dropping them on the floor. You'd think they didn't know how to get back from the bathroom without a trail of socks marking the way.

Drew and I, on the other hand, keep our personal areas organized. I figure, if you don't make a mess, you don't have to clean it up. Drew sweeps and mops the floor while I scrub the shower, clean the sink, and put a fresh coat of polish on the bathroom fixtures. I never had to do this kind of thing at home, but I did when I had my own place, and I don't mind the work.

When the Warden comes through to inspect our cabins, she is literally wearing white gloves to check for dust in the windowsills and dirt on the floor. To her surprise, and ours, she's happy with the results and takes pity on the fact that we've been stuck in our cabins most of the day. She drops by the chow hall while we're eating dinner and announces that our reward is a movie night in the barn after evening chores. It's incredible how hard up you get for a little entertainment when you haven't even seen a TV in months.

Drew and I walk up to the barn a few steps ahead of Seth and Todd, who are arguing over who left track marks in the toilet when they got back from dinner.

"Anyone know what movie we're watching?" Drew asks.

I don't know the answer, but if I have to sit through another showing of "My Name is Bill W.," I'll claw my eyes out. Don't get me wrong—it's a great story about two hopeless alcoholics who create a support group based on spiritual principles that allows them to find and maintain sobriety. After discovering that a spiritual awakening gives them the strength they need to overcome their illness, they take their message to other alcoholics and help them start on their path to recovery. (12 steps, n.d.) It's the true story of Bill W., Dr. Bob, and the conception of Alcoholics Anonymous.

There's no doubt in my mind that James Woods deserves the Oscar he won for playing Bill W. in the made-for-TV drama. Still, he and James Garner are relics of the era in which all movies were black and white. As a result, it's hard for some of us younger people to relate to the characters in the film, especially when watching it for the sixth or seventh time.

"I think it's that older movie with Denzel Washington in it." Seth says.

"Which one? The Bone Collector? Crimson Tide? Training Day?

"No. It's something called Flight."

"*Flight?*" Never heard of it."

"Well, it's better than folding underwear."

"That's for sure."

The barn is set up for an audience with those cheap, plastic lawn chairs you can buy for about ten dollars apiece. They aren't the kind you can recline in, but it's better than sitting on the ground—especially since this is the barn where I saw that snake the day after I arrived.

All the chairs face a portable movie screen, the kind that unrolls from the bottom and attaches to a hanger about five feet up for support. The projector is a cheap brand that probably costs under a hundred dollars. I'm pretty sure it all came from Walmart, but it's better than what we have in our cabins.

I don't see the Warden anywhere, but Vanessa shows up and pretends she's on a date with Drew. She sits right next to him and flirts with him the entire movie. I've never seen anything like it, but I do my best to ignore it. Besides, I'm happy sitting next to Erika.

None of the cowboys show up, but I don't know if the Warden invited them. So it's just us recovering addicts and a woman twice our age having a mid-life crisis sitting in a barn on a Friday night watching a ten-year-old movie that most of us have never heard of. I figure I'll probably sleep through the movie, but the opening scene grabs my attention like a bullhorn.

Denzel Washington is an airline pilot and wakes up next to a gorgeous flight attendant he slept with the night before. The first thing he does is snort a line of cocaine because he's the senior pilot on a commercial airliner scheduled to take off in less than an hour. Like a true addict, he has to get his head right to function at the start of the day.

The story is about how he saves nearly everyone on board by inverting a jet airliner upside down in flight because the horizontal stabilizer gets stuck in the down position. Although there are a few fatalities, including the flight attendant from the earlier scene, Denzel's character pulled off a miracle that no other pilot could have accomplished. As a result, the media hails him as a hero.

The subsequent investigation is where he runs into trouble because a blood test taken after the crash reveals that he had drugs and alcohol in his system when he miraculously landed the airplane. The main point of the story is that he had to come to terms with the fact that he's an alcoholic and broke the law by flying a passenger plane while completely loaded.

If you've never seen the movie, you have to see it. The screenplay was written by a recovering alcoholic and addict whose true-life events inspired the story. In fact, he received a nomination for an Academy Award for Best Original Screenplay. Denzel Washington was also nominated for an Academy Award for his performance as the main character. I think he should've won the award for Best Actor—hands down.

As the story progresses, Denzel's character tries to quit drinking because he knows he has to testify before the National Transportation Safety Board (NTSB), who is conducting the accident investigation. Still, he has bottles of alcohol hidden throughout the house, and he cannot stay sober—no matter what.

I don't know how many times I poured out every bottle of alcohol I had before getting "triggered" to drink again. Then, just like in the movie, I tore the entire house apart until I found a bottle I'd stashed so that no one knew about my drinking problem.

In one scene, Denzel's character drives to the liquor store and buys a bottle of booze. Instead of waiting until he gets home to open it, he starts chugging it right there in the liquor store parking lot. Been there—done that.

Okay—"spoiler alert!" The most powerful scene in the movie is when his handlers from the pilot's union, who *know* that he's a full-blown alcoholic, sequester him in a hotel room the night before the hearing so that he can't sabotage his own defense by getting loaded. In fact, they go to extreme lengths to protect him, from himself, including removing every bottle of alcohol from the mini-bar in his room and putting a guard outside to make sure he doesn't leave the room.

Denzel's character wakes up in the middle of the night because he hears a door creaking in the adjoining hotel room where someone left a window open. He finds that the connecting door is unlocked and enters the room to shut the window. But the only problem is, he notices the mini-bar in the corner of that room and finds it is fully stocked. True to the character of any realistic alcoholic, he is powerless over his disease and drinks every single bottle he can find.

I won't give away any more of the story, but I've never seen an actor play the part of an alcoholic or addict so authentically. The denial, the lies, and the insanity of it all are so realistic that I feel like the movie is a portrayal of my life—(except that I've never flown an airplane).

When the movie ends, I'm the last one to leave, not because I'm afraid of the rain, but because the message was so powerful. There's another saying in recovery circles that says, "nothing changes if nothing changes," and that's what Denzel's character finally realizes. Unless he surrenders to his disease, he will never overcome his addiction to drugs and alcohol.

* * * * * *

On my way back to the cabin, I see Drew standing alone on the pier in the pouring rain. Getting wet again doesn't sound fun to me, but Drew is my friend. So I have to make sure everything's okay.

"I had a cousin named Roy," he said, "that I grew up with in Salt Lake City. We were the same age and really close. He loved horses too, and we always talked about owning a ranch together someday."

"Roy had a heart condition and was overweight. He tried dieting, working out, weight loss surgery, but nothing worked. So when he heard about this new product called Metaphix, he talked to a doctor about it and decided to give it a try."

When Drew mentions Metaphix, my heart skips a beat. I know what he's about to say, and it hurts just to sit there and listen. There's no way I can tell him that my father invented Metaphix and that my family is ridiculously wealthy because of it.

"Roy did well with the first two injections, and he lost 45 pounds in 60 days. However, during the third injection, he suffered a heart attack and died right there on the doctor's table."

"Did he have a bad reaction to Metaphix?" I ask, knowing the answer before I ask it.

"Yeah, the doctor said he had an underlying heart condition that he didn't disclose, and he died because of the way the drug increases the heart rate to burn calories. His family sued the company that made Metaphix, and a federal court is about to make a ruling in the wrongful death lawsuit within the next few weeks."

"My aunt and uncle not only lost their son, but they've spent every dollar they had on attorney fees. If they don't get something out of the lawsuit, they'll have lost everything."

I remember hearing about this lawsuit a couple of years ago, not just because it involved my father's company but because it was all over the news. The company's shareholders panicked and sold off millions of investors' shares. They've mostly recovered, thanks to Metaphlex, but the market shares will bottom out again if Coleman Pharmaceutical Laboratories loses the class-action lawsuit.

I wish I could tell Drew everything will be okay, but I know my father. He will lie, steal, and cheat to save his company, and the attorneys that work for him will do even worse.

Maybe it's a good thing Drew is about to go home. I'll surely miss him, but if he ever found out who my father is, it would destroy our friendship and both of our souls.

CHAPTER 9

The rain doesn't stop for three days, which is unusual for Central Washington. Cities like Wenatchee and Ellensburg don't see more than 7 to 12 inches of precipitation a year, including the wetter winter months when snow falls for days. In fact, Central Washington boasts over 300 days of sunshine a year. However, no one at the Washington Tourism Bureau ever mentions that the wind can be blowing 65 miles per hour, and there will not be a cloud in the sky.

The power company came out and repaired the downed power line, so the power was only out for about 12 hours. But, unfortunately, the power outage prevented the security cameras from recording any video of a truck and trailer coming or going from the ranch.

Pit Bull is sure it's either Goodman, the guy who ran us off the road, or one of his sons. He said he would inform the Warden and file a police report, but from what I know about Pit Bull, he's more likely to ride straight over to Goodman's ranch, start shooting, and ask questions later.

For the most part, we are limited in what we can do outside due to the weather. It's not that there aren't chores to do on a ranch when the weather is foul, but they don't always require the entire team to accomplish them.

For example, we don't have to move irrigation pipes because all the fields are getting watered. And no one is out cutting the hay either because that would be stupid, according to Todd. Bailing wet hay can result in mold, and unintentional fires, as strange as that may sound. Bacterial growth can raise temperatures in even the driest bales of hay. When the internal temperature of hay rises above 130 degrees Fahrenheit, a chemical reaction can occur that produces flammable gases.

Since we rounded up all the cattle and brought them closer in, we just have to make sure we put out enough hay to balance their diet. The calving season just finished, so all we really need to do is ride out each day and make sure there aren't any sick or injured cows.

The prison guards work on projects that have been sitting around waiting for days like this. One is a decent mechanic, so he's working on a hay baler that seized up due to a broken oil line. Another is sharpening blades on the hay mowers, and a couple of others are inspecting belts and performing other routine maintenance necessary to keep ranch equipment running.

As for us inmates, we mostly keep to ourselves and take advantage of the time off. That doesn't mean we don't work—there are always cows to feed, stalls to clean, and that sort of thing. But sometimes, I feel they are making up chores for us just to keep us busy.

For instance, we moved a stack of hay bales from one end of the barn to the other. Why that was necessary, I have no idea. We also had to clean the chicken coop floor, which was almost as bad as the day I spent cleaning the slaughterhouse.

When I'm not working, I spend time with Erika. Sometimes we play cards or board games, and other times we just talk. Right now, Seth is the reigning UNO champion, but I think he cheats.

Erika grew up in Boise, Idaho, but moved to Vancouver to attend school at the University of Portland, four and a half miles away. However, her family still lives in Boise, and she says it's a great place to grow up.

She's the oldest of three girls, but she grew up playing competitive sports. As a result, she thinks of herself as a "tom-boy." I'll tell you what, though, when I look at her, I don't see anything "boyish."

We both enjoy running. Erika ran cross-country in high school and started running marathons when she moved to Vancouver. I didn't run cross-country but started running more after Nate died. I've run five marathons, but never an ultramarathon. I don't even think I'd want to run that far.

Erika says she prefers half-marathons but wants to train for another full marathon as part of her recovery plan. It's a great idea, but it's been a long time since I even thought about running.

She asked me how I got into running marathons, so I entertained her while the rain fell outside.

*****

It was an unseasonably crisp Saturday morning in September, just two weeks after starting my freshman year of high school. It was tryouts for the Bellevue High School Track Team, and I'd looked forward to this day for several months.

It was perfect running weather in Bellevue, the kind of morning where you wake up and think, "This is going to be my day!" So when the starting gun went off, I sprinted into the front of the pack and left every other runner in my dust.

I was ecstatic that I had a 20-yard lead on the closest runner halfway through the lap. And even though I had a searing pain in my chest, I maintained that lead the entire way around the track. Unfortunately, I realized a bit late that my pace was too fast. I was trying out for the 1600-meter event and had three more laps to go.

My legs faded halfway into the second lap when Brooks Larson passed me, followed shortly by Logan Kemp, Dillon McDermott, Duke Kiona, Noah Thomas, Dex Clark, and Lex Stuart. I don't know who else passed me because, by that time, my lungs were on fire, and I wasn't getting enough blood to my brain to see straight.

Just for the record books, I was the 1st of 18 runners to finish the 1st lap, but I was the 18th of 18 runners to complete the 4th lap. I was humiliated.

Coach Samson was not at all surprised when Brooks Larson crossed the finish line in 4:35.64. He'd already proven himself a distinguished miler. He would win the state championship two years later, in his senior year, before being offered an athletic scholarship to Stanford University. But for me, well, that one 1600-meter race nearly ended my running career.

The problem was, I loved to run. So after taking the rest of my freshman year off, I started running again in the summer between my freshman and sophomore years. Though not competitive, I became a decent runner before drugs took over my life.

My first race was a 5-miler put on by a local running club. It wasn't a big race, only about 400 entrants from all age groups. Some of the runners were old, thin, and wiry, while others were young and inexperienced. There were moms, dads, children in jogger strollers, high school students, and even an Army battalion running in formation.

In the early part of the race, I felt good. I loved the feeling of the wind in my face and the energy of bodies in motion. I also enjoyed the camaraderie and the unspoken goal of wanting to beat every other runner out there.

At the two-and-a-half-mile turnaround, I got to see the other runners, and it thrilled me to see people laughing, smiling, and motivating each other to give their best effort. For almost a mile, I got so caught up with all the excitement that I didn't even realize how much it hurt.

As the 4th mile approached, the pain in my legs and lungs grew worse. My legs felt dead and I could feel my lungs burning. Aside from that I started to feel dizzy, but there was no way I was slowing or stopping. In the final half-mile of the race, I pushed myself even harder, passing more experienced and better-trained athletes right up to the finish. As a reward for my efforts, I finished first in my age group and seventh overall.

Propelled by such a stunning finish, I decided to increase the distance and push myself harder in the next race. Since a 5K race was a shorter distance than I'd just run, and a 10K was only 1.2 miles further, I signed up for the very next race I could find longer than a 10K. I signed up for the Seattle marathon.

When my other running friends said that attempting a marathon with only six months of running experience was suicidal, I didn't think twice about it. I signed up for the Seattle Marathon—3 months, 11 days away, and I found a training plan I found online to prepare for it. My mindset was simple—follow the plan, and I'd be ready. But, of course, with less than 20 full weeks to train, I did have to condense my training schedule a tiny bit.

The training plan instructed me to supplement my regular runs of 3-4 miles per day, three days a week, with an ever-increasing long run on the weekend. The author said the long run helps build endurance, but adding too much, too quickly, would likely result in an injury.

On Monday, Wednesday, and Friday, I ran my usual 3-4 miles, taking the other days off from running, except for Sunday. Each Sunday was my "long-run," which started at 8 miles and increased by 2 miles each week. The goal of the training plan was to get up to run a 20-miler exactly two weeks before race day.

My first *long* run was a challenging 8 miles. It took a little over an hour, and I was utterly spent at the end of it. I'd never run that far or that long, and by the time I finished, I had blisters on both feet and couldn't walk up the stairs for two days.

After buying a good pair of running shoes from a running store that analyzed my gait and the wear patterns of my old shoes, I solved the blister problem, but I had to accept that I would have to put in the necessary training to build my running endurance. I had to trust that the training plan would get me ready, especially when, at the end of the 20-week program, I should "be able to run comfortably for at least three hours." (I laughed out loud when I read that!)

I had no idea how long it would take to complete a marathon, but I figured, mathematically, that if I kept a pace of 6 minutes, 50 seconds per mile, I would finish in just under three hours. So running a sub-three-hour marathon became my goal. It never occurred to me that just *finishing* a marathon was an admirable goal for any first-timer.

My training plan had me running my last long run precisely two weeks before race day. That run would be 20 miles. The article said that if I followed the plan, completed a 20-mile run two weeks out, and conserved my strength from that point until race day, "the crowd effect and adrenaline [would] carry [me] the remaining 6.2 miles to the finish line."

I felt amazing on race day as I toed the start line with the other 1,486 runners—so amazing that I started out on a 6:30 pace per mile. I knew it was too fast, but the cheering crowd, the adrenaline in my blood, and the thrill that race day had *finally* arrived were electrifying.

At 10 miles in, I was 2 minutes ahead of where I expected to be at this point in the race. However, my exuberance at the start of the race exceeded my metabolic output, and my pace slowed to 6:45 per mile. At 13.1 miles, I was running 7:00 per mile, and I recorded a time of 1 hour, 29 minutes, and 48 seconds for the first half of the marathon.

My mind quickly calculated my pace over the remaining distance. If I could get back on a 6:55 per mile pace, I could still finish in under 3 hours. So, digging deep, I sped up enough to clock a 6:52 split the next mile and two 6:53 splits for miles 15 and 16. After that, it took more and more effort to maintain a sub-7-minute per mile pace.

At mile 18, my first cramp hit me like a school bus. *What is that?* I screamed in my head. It felt like someone had shot me in the leg, and I had to stop to ensure it was sweat dripping down my leg and not blood.

As soon as I started running again, the cramp returned, this time even tighter. I stopped and looked at my right calf muscle and could see it spasming like something was burrowing under my skin. In my entire 9-month running career, I'd never experienced anything like it.

I'd seen others alongside the course stretching their calves, so I limped over to the sidewalk and tried to stretch mine. It was the first time I'd stopped moving in over two hours, and a little girl standing nearby asked her father why I was trying to push over a light pole. After 30 seconds in that position, the cramp subsided, but so did my goal of finishing a sub-three-hour marathon.

Over the next three miles, I walked a hundred yards, jogged a hundred yards, then walked another hundred yards—over, and over, and over again. That cramp continued to plague me to the point that I eventually couldn't run at all.

Moving at a turtle's pace, I walked up to the aid station at mile 22 and stopped in front of a table with small green cups of clear and yellow fluids. A young twelve- or thirteen-year-old girl held out one of the half-filled green cups in front of her.

"You're doing great!" she cheered. "Just four miles to go!"

"*What did you say?*" I growled.

"J-just f-four miles to go," she repeated, this time with less conviction.

I stared at the cup in her hands for several seconds before realizing I was supposed to drink it. Up to this point, I'd ignored all previous aid stations under the assumption that filling up with fluids would only slow me down. There were also plates with bananas cut in thirds and oranges cut into slices. The other runners were taking the green cups with them as they ran, drinking them mid-stride.

When my head finally cleared enough to realize why I was cramping, I grabbed a cup of Gatorade in one hand, water in the other, and gulped them down like I'd just eaten a handful of ghost peppers. After two more cups and a half-dozen bananas, I started toward the finish line and heaved everything in my stomach on the legs of a very fit and attractive woman running by.

The woman screamed and stopped in her tracks, turning slowly to stare at the bits of banana dripping down her calves. All I could do was stare back in disbelief and apologize over and over again.

A slew of aid station volunteers surrounded the woman and ushered her toward a hose used to cool off runners. I just hoped she wasn't the lead female runner or someone contending for a podium spot because she wasn't smiling for any pictures.

Those last four miles felt like four hundred miles. Step by step, I shuffled toward the finish line with both legs now under full-cramp assault. I stopped at nearly every street corner to stretch my legs on the nearest curb, parking block, or light pole I could find.

The only thing that hurt worse than my legs that day was my pride. I inched my way to the finish line with my head down. Runners I'd passed earlier in the race blew by me like I was standing still. It was the most humbling experience of my life.

At the finish, after 3 hours, 41 minutes on the course, I crossed the line and collapsed into the arms of a volunteer. The last 6.2 miles had taken me nearly as long as it took me to run the first half of the marathon.

Later that night, I couldn't even remember how I got to my car and drove home. I slept for several hours and ate a bowl of chicken noodle soup with an extra tablespoon of salt to replace the sodium I sweated out.

When I finished telling Erika the story, she asked, "How were you able to finish?"

"I just had to keep moving my feet," I said, "one step at a time."

There's a saying in recovery circles that says, "easy does it—one day at a time. Rather than thinking about a lifetime of sobriety all at once, maybe I just need to keep taking forward steps—one step at a time. In the end, those little steps will add up to miles.

CHAPTER 10

By the time the rain stops, I have cabin fever so bad I'm climbing the walls. Everyone is ready to get out and do something besides tell stories and play UNO.

The Warden came by to take money and orders for the weekly cigarette run, but I've decided to quit smoking. Like every other addiction, it begins to control your life. I was on a 14-hour non-stop flight to Paris one time and thought I was going to die. Besides, Erika talked me into training for another marathon when we get out of here, and there's no way I want to run a marathon with a two-pack-a-day habit. More importantly, however, I can't let her beat me.

I asked the Warden about the missing cattle and the tire tracks, but she pretended she didn't know anything about it. It surprised me because Pit Bull said they would file a police report. So maybe she forgot about it, or he hasn't had a chance to tell her. Either way, it surprised me that no one had reported it.

Pit Bull has left us alone for the most part. He tells us what to do but leaves the "eyes-on" supervision to the prison guards. For the most part, they're all pretty good guys. I get along with them because they're just trying to keep busy and stay clean like the rest of us.

Ranching is pretty good work when you need to keep out of trouble. At least it's honest work, and I don't mind getting dirty anymore.

We spend most of the day checking fences and roads to ensure the storm didn't wash anything away. The fences look good, but we have to clear some blocked drainage ditches and one section of the road that washed away. Drew, Todd, and I reposition a fence line so that we can drive around the washout until Pit Bull can get a backhoe up there to fix it.

Seth got pimped out to the slaughterhouse, but he doesn't seem to mind too much. He says the cruelty doesn't bother him. There might just be something to what Drew said about him lighting a dog on fire.

* * * * *

It's a meeting night, and as much as it pains me, I'm sitting on the floor next to Erika, unable to get comfortable. My butt still isn't accustomed to sitting in a saddle all day.

It's Drews turn to lead the meeting, and he surprises everyone with a question. "Would anyone mind if we used a slightly different format to open our meeting tonight?"

"How do you mean?" I ask. "Do we still take turns sharing?"

"Of course," Drew says. "It's really just a change to what is said at the beginning of the meeting. It still follows the 12-step format we're all familiar with, but there is a slight change in some of the wording."

"I've been involved in this program for about five months because it emphasizes the spiritual side of recovery. It focuses more directly on Jesus Christ as our Redeemer and Savior. It's changed the way I look at addiction. I'm wondering if anyone else might benefit from it."

I'm wary of introducing something new, but I decide that if it's really possible to have a personal relationship with God, then maybe something good will come of it.

"Fine with me," I say, looking around the room for any objections. No one seems to have any, or at least they don't voice them.

"Okay, cool," Drew says, "if anyone feels uncomfortable with this format, just speak up, and we'll go back to the standard opening."

"Hi, my name is Drew, and I'm an addict." He pauses and waits for the expected return greeting from attendees.

"Hi, Drew."

"Welcome to the Serenity Ranch addiction recovery meeting. Can we open this meeting with a word of prayer?"

No one opposes starting with prayer, but I don't hear anyone volunteer, either.

Drew surprises me when he asks, "Jake, would you mind saying a prayer for us?"

"I, uh, I've n-never said a prayer in public." I stammer. "I wouldn't know how."

"It's easy," Drew says, realizing that some of us don't know how to pray. "We just address our Heavenly Father, tell Him what we are thankful for, ask Him for what we need, and close in the name of Jesus Christ, amen."

"I'll try," I reply, suddenly just as nervous as I was riding a horse. My nervousness subsides when Erika takes my hand in hers, but then I realize that everyone is holding hands in a big circle on the floor.

"Heavenly Father," I begin, after closing my eyes like everyone else. "Thank you for this day. And thank you for giving us this time to meet together and help each other conquer our addictions. Please help us know what we need to do to get past our struggles with drugs and alcohol."

I forget what comes next and start to look at Drew when Erika whispers to me, "In the name of Jesus Christ."

"…in the name of Jesus Christ, amen."

"Thank you, Jake," Drew says. "That was perfect."

Everyone relaxes and settles into the meeting, but neither Erika nor I let go of each other's hands. I don't know if it's her touch or the fact that I just said my first public prayer, but I feel a peace come over me that I've never felt before. It's a happy feeling, and one I haven't felt in a very long time.

Drew opens a spiral-bound booklet with the title Addiction Recovery Program and begins reading:

> We have known great sorrow, but we have seen the power of the Savior turn our most devastating defeats into glorious spiritual victories. We who once lived with daily depression, anxiety, fear, and debilitating anger now experience joy and peace. We have witnessed miracles in our own lives and in the lives of others who were ensnared in addiction.
>
> We have paid an awful price in self-inflicted pain and suffering because of our addictions. But blessings have poured forth as we have taken each step to recovery. Having had a spiritual awakening, we strive every day to improve our relationship with Heavenly Father and His Son, Jesus Christ. Through the Atonement of Jesus Christ, we are healed.
>
> We invite you with all our empathy and love to join us in a glorious life of freedom and safety, encircled in the arms of Jesus Christ, our Redeemer. We know by our own experience that you can break free from the chains of addiction. No matter how lost and hopeless you may feel, you are the child of a loving Heavenly Father. If you have been blind to this truth, the principles explained in this guide will help you rediscover it and establish it deep in your heart. These principles can help you come unto Christ and allow Him to change you. As you apply the principles, you will draw on the power of the Atonement, and the Lord will free you from bondage.
>
> Some people consider addictions to be simply bad habits that can be conquered by willpower alone, but

many people become so dependent on a behavior or a substance that they no longer see how to abstain from it. They lose perspective and a sense of other priorities in their lives. Nothing matters more than satisfying their desperate need. When they try to abstain, they experience powerful physical, psychological, and emotional cravings. As they habitually make wrong choices, they find their ability to choose the right diminished or restricted. As President Boyd K. Packer of the Quorum of the Twelve Apostles taught, "Addiction has the capacity to disconnect the human will and nullify moral agency. It can rob one of the power to decide."[7]

Addictions can include the use of substances such as tobacco, alcohol, coffee, tea, and drugs (both prescription and illegal), and behaviors such as gambling, codependency, viewing pornography, inappropriate sexual behavior, and disorders associated with eating. These substances and behaviors diminish a person's ability to feel the Spirit. They harm physical and mental health and social, emotional, and spiritual well-being.

Elder Dallin H. Oaks of the Quorum of the Twelve taught, "We should avoid any behavior that is addictive. Whatever is addictive compromises our will. Subjecting our will to the overbearing impulses imposed by any form of addiction serves Satan's purposes and subverts our Heavenly Father's. This applies to addictions to drugs (such as narcotics, alcohol, nicotine, or caffeine), addiction to practices such as gambling, and any other addictive behavior. We can avoid addictions by keeping the commandments of God."[8]

---

[7] Packer, Boyd K., *Ensign*, (Salt Lake City: The Church of Jesus Christ of Latter-day Saints, Nov. 1989), 14.

[8] Oaks, Dallin H., "Free Agency and Freedom," *Brigham Young University 1987-88 Devotional and Fireside Speeches* [1988], 45.

By being humble and honest and calling upon God and others for help, you can overcome your addictions through the Atonement of Jesus Christ. Just as we have recovered, you can recover and enjoy all the blessings of the gospel of Jesus Christ.

If you suspect you are addicted and if you feel even the smallest desire to break free, we invite you to join us in studying and applying the principles of the gospel of Jesus Christ as they are taught in this guide. We assure you that if you follow this path with a sincere heart, you will find the power you need to recover from addiction. As you apply each of these twelve principles faithfully, the Savior will strengthen you, and you will come to "know the truth, and the truth shall make you free" (John 8:32).[9]

While Drew was reading, some of the principles he shared really grabbed my attention. First, he said that *no matter how lost and hopeless we may feel, we are all children of a loving Heavenly Father.* That is a powerful statement, and though it describes how I've felt for many years, it gives me hope that things can be different.

Second, he said that it is *through the Atonement of Jesus Christ that we are healed.* The concept of Jesus Christ as our Savior is not new to me. I just haven't felt that his healing power *applied* to me—at least not on a personal level.

Third, he said that *addiction is not a lack of willpower or simply bad habits. Our addictions take away our ability to choose and our agency to decide.* Addiction is a lot like being in prison—the freedom to choose is no longer your own.

---

[9] LDS Family Services, Addiction Recovery Program: A Guide to Addiction Recovery and Healing, (Salt Lake City: The Church of Jesus Christ of Latter-day Saints, 2005), *v-vi*.

Fourth, he said that we can *find the power to overcome addiction by studying and applying the principles of the Gospel of Jesus Christ.* If that's true, maybe there is something I can get out of this program.

Drew continues. "Monica, would you please read the 12 steps to recovery?"

As she begins reading, I finally realize how much this program is based on having genuine faith in God—not in a tree or in a doorknob—but in a loving Father in Heaven who wants us to be happy, not miserable.

> Step 1: *Honesty* - Admit that you, of yourself, are powerless to overcome your addiction and that your life has become unmanageable.
>
> Step 2: *Hope* - Come to believe that the power of God can restore you to complete spiritual health.
>
> Step 3: *Trust in God* - Decide to turn your will and your life over to the care of God the Eternal Father and His Son, Jesus Christ.
>
> Step 4: *Truth* - Make a searching and fearless written moral inventory of yourself.
>
> Step 5: *Confession* - Admit to yourself, to your Heavenly Father in the name of Jesus Christ, to proper priesthood authority, and to another person the exact nature of your wrongs.
>
> Step 6: *Change of Heart* - Become entirely ready to have God remove all your character weaknesses.
>
> Step 7: *Humility* - Humbly ask Heavenly Father to remove your shortcomings.

Step 8: *Seeking Forgiveness* - Make a written list of all persons you have harmed and become willing to make restoration to them.

Step 9: *Restitution and Reconciliation* - Wherever possible, make direct restitution to all persons you have harmed.

Step 10: *Daily Accountability* - Continue to take personal inventory, and when you are wrong, promptly admit it.

Step 11: *Personal Revelation* - Seek through prayer and meditation to know the Lord's will and to have the power to carry it out.

Step 12: *Service* - Having had a spiritual awakening as a result of the Atonement of Jesus Christ, share this message with others and practice these principles in all you do.[10]

When Monica finishes reading, Drew is the first to share.
"My name is Drew, and I'm a sex addict."
I almost start to laugh, thinking Drew is trying to be funny, but when I see the tear in his eye, I catch myself. Erika and I both look at each other, as do others in the room. Everyone knows that Drew is here because he told his parents he was addicted to drugs.
"I can't live the lie I've been living any longer," he says. "It's time for me to be honest and tell you why I'm really here."
"I was introduced to pornography when I was nine years old. A kid at school brought a magazine from home full of pictures of naked men and women.
I didn't know at the time that it was pornography, but I knew the instant I saw it that it wasn't good. I knew it wasn't something I

---
[10] LDS Family Services, *Addiction Recovery Program*, iv

should be around, but the pictures also made me curious. Later that night, I couldn't get the images out of my head, no matter how hard I tried."

"A few years later, I was at a sleepover with some friends, and we started watching a movie that I'd heard some of them talking about at school. It wasn't a movie that I'd ever thought about watching, but what I saw on TV aroused feelings inside of me I'd never had before. It was all about sex, and, like a magnet, it pulled me in."

"When I was home alone, I started looking at pornography online and fantasizing about seeing a woman naked and having sex. I really didn't know much about sex at that time, but it didn't take long before I knew more than I wanted to know, and I couldn't stop thinking about it."

"By the time I discovered masturbation, I was into hard-core pornography, and it was starting to affect my life. I knew it was improper because it made me feel extremely shameful and full of remorse. I felt dirty, unworthy, and undeserving of God's love."

"I tried to stay away from it, but I was addicted and spent more and more time alone, in my room, filling my head with the vilest images imaginable. Finally, it consumed me to the point that I thought about taking my own life."

"Things finally got bad enough that I decided I just had to get away from my friends and the internet, and any exposure at all to pornography. So I started looking for help with addiction, and I read about Serenity Ranch."

"I was home from school one weekend, and I came up with this plan to make my parents believe I was using drugs. I've never used drugs in my life, but like here, I was too embarrassed to tell them about my real issues."

"I'm here because I need help. I know that if I don't figure out how to address my addiction, I'll do straight back to it as soon as I get home."

"I have made a lot of progress over the last five months, and I've felt our Heavenly Father's love for me as I've started praying and rereading the scriptures. I don't think I'm cured, but I know I'm in a better place and on a better path than before."

"I talked to my bishop about things before I came out here, and he told me that our church has its own addiction recovery program, patterned after the 12-step program used in A.A. He even gave me this manual I've been reading, and today marks six months that I've been clean."

The tears running down Drew's face have been collecting on his shirt, and he looks like someone hit him with a water balloon. I've never heard of anyone having an addiction to pornography, but I know Drew's pain is just as real as my own.

"Just the other day, I had my biggest test when Vanessa cornered me in the barn. It was like having a fantasy play out in real life, but I knew if I gave in to temptation, I'd be right back where I started.

I just kept thinking of the story in the Bible about Joseph and Potiphar's wife. Potiphar's wife made sexual advances toward him, but the scriptures tell us he 'fled and got him[self] out.' So I ran out of that barn faster than I've ever run in my life. And you know what? It felt great!"

"Anyway," he says, "I needed to come clean, and I hope you guys know how sorry I am that I lied to you all this time. I hope you can find it in your hearts to forgive me."

When the meeting adjourns, every person in the room walks up to Drew and gives him the biggest hugs they possibly can. It's a little past 8:00, but no one cares. It's evident from the smile on Drew's face that he just unloaded a massive weight off his shoulders. I'm glad he's in a better place. I think I've made a breakthrough myself, and I'd like to join him on that "better path."

CHAPTER 11

The Big Book says that our thoughts, feelings, and beliefs are the roots of our addictive behaviors. One of the most significant obstacles we face as addicts and alcoholics is that most of our problems reside in that six-inch space between our ears. Let's face it—drugs screw with your brain, and our mental processes are in complete disarray.

For example, Addiction counselors teach us to identify when we have negative thought patterns. They call this "stinking thinking." Stinking thinking occurs when we don't see the good in our lives, see nothing but obstacles in our path, or believe that failure is inevitable. To overcome these mental barriers, we have to change the way we think.

Addiction is also an incredibly shameful disease—if you think of it as a *disease*. Many people don't. They look at it as a problem with willpower or self-discipline. My parents think that way, even my mother, but then, of course, she can't even admit that she's an alcoholic.

Those who believe that addiction is a disease recognize that it's really a disease of the mind—one that denigrates our thinking processes and makes us dependent on drugs.

Addiction is looked upon differently than diseases like cancer, diabetes, or heart disease. For lack of better words, those diseases are, unfortunate, but *honorable* diseases—the kind where fate picked you out of a crowd, not where you did something to deserve it.

Addiction is one of the diseases people have difficulty showing sympathy toward, like getting lung cancer from smoking or liver disease from excess alcohol consumption. It's the same for addictions to gambling or pornography—addiction is viewed as a moral problem, not misfortune. For this reason, addicts view themselves as failures, weak, and unworthy of love.

For the past week, I've been working on my Step 4, and it is one of the most humbling things I've ever done. Step 4 is where we conduct a searching and fearless moral inventory of ourselves. Its purpose is to identify negative thoughts, emotions, and actions that *rule* our lives. We do our best to determine the root causes of our addictive behaviors because our behaviors, drinking and drugging, are only symptoms of a more profound character defect.

I talked to Erika about doing my Step 4, and she was surprised I hadn't done one already. After all, this *is* my fifth time in rehab. She encouraged me to take my time and ask myself what part I played in events that led to self-destructive behavior. It's pretty easy to blame others for the things we do, but how we react to events is often our biggest downfall—not the events themselves.

As I've been taking my moral inventory, I've discovered all kinds of things I didn't know about myself. Since it's not a meeting night, I told her I would be done by tonight and wanted to share it with her as part of my Step 5.

It's a little past 7:00 PM when we finish the evening chores. I can already see Erika sitting on the pier waiting for me. I stop by the cabin and get my notebook and start walking down to the pier. I reach for a cigarette out of habit, but my pocket is empty, and I remember that I quit smoking. That sucks! I could really use one right about now.

"Hey, she says, when she hears the sounds of my boots on the wooden boards, "how was your day?"

"It was okay. Nothing too exciting; we just cleaned out some ditches and worked on some fences. How was yours?"

"Good," she says, always with a smile. "We got the truck stuck in the mud. It was so much fun! By the time we got it out, we had more mud on us than there was on the truck."

"I thought that truck had 4-wheel drive."

"It *does,* but when you go muddin' after as much rain as we've had, even a 4-wheel drive can get stuck, especially when the mud is up to the wheel wells."

"Wow! That's crazy!"

"Yeah. We had a blast getting it stuck. Pit Bull had to bring down a tractor to pull us out," she says, laughing. "He was *so* mad. He made us clean both the truck and the tractor, but it was worth it—not just gettin' stuck, but seein' him get so mad."

I sit down next to her and open my notebook. "Should we get this over with?"

"Whenever you're ready, Jake. You don't have to rush through this. I'm here whenever you want to talk. And remember, I'm not going to judge you. Steps 4 and 5 are opportunities to clean house—get rid of all the baggage you've been carrying around."

"I don't even know where to start," I say, looking at the chart I made and the things that fell out of my head onto the paper.

"Start wherever you'd like."

"Well, I made a chart," I say, a little bit embarrassed that my entire life boils down to a page with a half-dozen columns.

"Charts are good," Erika responds with a bit of surprise in her voice.

"I broke it down into four elements: the incidents, the effects, the feelings, and the lessons learned."

"Okay, great," Erika says, "You did put some thought into this, didn't you?"

"Well," I say, "I've tried this a couple of other times with a sponsor, and it never really worked for me. So, I think I was doing it just because someone told me I had to. But, I really want it to work this time."

"That's great, Jake. I hope it does too."

I start by telling Erika about the relationship I had with my family before the accident. I'd forgotten how close my father and I were at one point. He really was someone I admired and tried to emulate, but our relationship fell apart when Nate drowned in the Yakima River.

When I think about that day, I feel like I'm going to throw up. The pain is real. The guilt is indescribable. I've always blamed myself for not being able to save Nate. He was right there in front of me, an arm's reach away, yet I didn't get to him. I should have swum harder, kicked harder, held my breath longer—anything that could have saved him—but I didn't, and that's why I feel responsible for Nate's death.

I didn't know how to deal with it any other way. So instead of telling my parents, or anyone else, what I was feeling, I bottled it all up inside. Like cancer, it ate my soul. I know it's the primary reason I turned to drugs and alcohol—I don't need a shrink or a sponsor to tell me that. I need someone to tell me how to live with it because, if not, it's going to kill me.

My father saved *me* that day and not my brother. If he had the choice, he would have saved Nate—he's told me that many times. He said that I should have known better than to let water get into my waders. He said I should have done more for Nate. He blames me because he isn't strong enough to take responsibility himself.

My mother never said that she holds me responsible, but she's never told me she doesn't. Instead, she just sits in her room and acts like neither Nate nor I ever existed.

As I tell Erika about my past, I feel a burden being lifted. They say that confession is good for the soul, and I'm becoming a believer. The crazy part is that I feel like I can tell Erika things I can't tell anyone else—not my parents, not a counselor, not even my sponsor, Kris. It's nice to have someone I feel comfortable around. It's been a long time since I've had someone like that in my life.

The truth is, something happened right before Nate died that I have not shared with anyone else in this world. I've felt guilty about it for years, and I know it's a big part of why I can't stay clean.

Nate and I got into an argument right before we got in the river to go fishing. I'd brought with me a two-liter bottle of Dr. Pepper and drank most of it on the drive from the campground. When we arrived, Nate realized he'd forgotten his vivarium back at camp.

If you don't know what a vivarium is, think of an aquarium for insects without the water. It's really just a plastic container with small vent holes that allow insects to breathe inside.

Nate brought one on the trip and collected a few bugs the first day, but he accidentally left it in the tent when we went fishing. Instead of telling my father and risking getting reprimanded, he poured out the rest of my Dr. Pepper and cut slits in the bottle with his pocketknife.

When I went back to the car to get my drink and found out what he'd done, I was angry and yelled at Nate. I knew he was sorry, but I was still mad; in fact, when he tried to apologize, I told him to "go to hell." That was the last thing I said to Nate before he drowned.

I cannot think back on that day and not hear those words echo through my head. They haunt me day and night. I feel like, somehow, I caused his death by saying what I said—which I know isn't true, but I have never been able to forgive myself.

The worst part was that I walked away from God when Nate died because I didn't think He could love me after that. Like what happened to Todd, I shut the door and locked Him out of my life. I realized now, I shouldn't have done that, but my downward spiral didn't end there.

The worst fight my father and I ever got into was when I started having disturbing memories of the night I got drunk on that ski trip when I was fifteen. For many years, I couldn't remember anything past going into the bathroom on the bus and puking my guts out, but a psychiatrist helped me uncover memories I now wish we'd left alone.

I was sexually assaulted the night I got drunk on the ASB Leadership ski trip—not by a student or a faculty advisor—by someone I knew and trusted. I remember being carried out of a car by someone and tucked in my bed. I still can't see a face in the bits of memory that surfaced, but I remember thinking that everything would be okay—and then it wasn't.

When the memories came back to me, I remember the person undressing me. Then I remember that person touching me in ways that made me feel uncomfortable. I don't think sex was involved, but there was inappropriate contact that I can only describe as sexual assault.

Not long ago, I got into an argument with my father about money. I needed to borrow some since he'd cut off my tuition and allowance. He said he wouldn't give me another dime and kept telling me that it was for my own good. He was right—he knew I'd buy drugs with it.

It was strange because he kept lashing out at me—kept telling me how he was finished bailing me out of trouble—that I needed to grow up and get a job. Then he recounted every single time he'd rescued me and tried to help me get off drugs.

One of the incidents he mentioned was how he picked me up from school one night after a ski trip when I was drunk. I had never spoken to *anyone* about that night, and the only way he could have known about it was by being there.

That was the night I went into his study and took a gun he kept in the bottom drawer. I was so upset that I swore I was going to kill him. The problem was that I couldn't do it. I knew I'd end up in prison for the rest of my life, so I put the gun to my own head and pulled the trigger.

Fortunately, there wasn't a round in the chamber, or the gun just didn't fire—I was too drunk to understand why the gun wouldn't work. I ended up running out to my car and crashing into a streetlight just a block from our house.

The paramedics rushed me to the hospital, but not because of any injuries—they couldn't understand how I was still alive with a blood alcohol content of 0.459. I was charged with a DUI, and true to his word, my father didn't bail me out.

That was my rock-bottom—the lowest point I could imagine hitting. After that, I couldn't live with the pain any longer and knew I had nothing else to lose. That was when I knew I had to get clean once and for all.

My conversation with Erika goes on for another forty-five minutes. I describe my character defects that aggravated and prolonged my illness. I can't go into full detail because it's a very confidential topic.

"Wow," Erika says when I finish talking. "I can't believe you went through all of that, Jake. I'm so sorry, but I think you've made some important discoveries about yourself, and I know that you're willing to take responsibility for the pain and sorrow you've caused others because of your actions."

She gives me a giant hug, and we just hold each other for a few minutes. I do feel much better, and it's not just because I'm in her arms. I've carried a boat anchor around for several years tied to my neck. Thankfully, it finally feels like I cut the rope.

I guess all I must do now is ask God to do His part and forgive me for the parts I played in this. Then, somehow, I must also forgive those who wronged me. That may be even harder than what I just did, but I'm taking things one day at a time.

*****

It's just a few minutes before 9:00 PM when I open the door and realize the lights in the cabin are already out. I hear Todd snoring in the bunk beneath mine. I don't know if everyone was tired and turned out the lights or if the Warden shut out the lights for some other reason.

SERENITY RANCH

I find my way to the bathroom and brush my teeth in the dark. Then, when I climb onto the top bunk, I hear Drew's ankle bones pop as he gets off his knees and crawls into his bed.

Instead of kneeling on the floor next to someone else's bed (because that would be really weird if Todd woke up and found me that way), I kneel on my mattress. I think God will understand.

Heavenly Father…I'm not sure how to do this, but I'm going to do the best I can. I've been here at the ranch for a while now, and I've had a chance to look at my life from a different perspective—at least one where I know that if I can't stay clean, I'm going to wind up dead or in jail. I don't have any other options.

Father, I've done my best to take a searching and fearless moral inventory, and I want to tell you what I've learned. You know what's happened in my life, so I don't think I need to go over them in detail like I did with Erika tonight, but I know that I haven't reacted well to some of these events and worsened the problems by blaming others.

When Nate died, I was angry for a very long time—angry at my father for making me feel responsible for Nate's death, angry at myself for not doing more to save him, and angry at you for letting Nate die.

I asked Drew why you would let bad things happen to good people when so many bad people are running around. He said that our lives are meant to challenge us—I think he called this life "a test"—and that you want to see whether we will be faithful and do the things you ask us to do.

Drew also said that Nate is with you now and that he's looking down on me and the mess I've made of my life. I don't think he's very proud of me, is he? I know he wouldn't be happy with my relationship with my parents. But, I now know that it wasn't anyone's fault that Nate died and that I can't blame myself or anyone else, especially not you. It was just part of life.

I also know that I can't change other people, and I can't change the past. I don't know why my father did what he did to me all those years ago, but I know people can work through that sort of thing and go on with their lives. I can't do that when every single thought about my father makes me want to die. There was a time that I loved him, and we all made mistakes. If there is a way you can help me forgive him, I think I'll have a better chance at staying sober.

When I wrote down my Step 4, I recognized a pattern to my behavior that I need to correct. When something terrible happens, I always look at myself as the victim and tell myself that I don't deserve what happened. That self-pity turns into resentment toward whoever wronged me, and my resentment turns into anger and rebellion, which is why I am an addict.

I also have an integrity problem. It's not just that I am willing to lie to anyone about anything, but I have never been a man of my word. There's no telling how many times I've promised to give up drugs only to break my word or promised to stay in treatment and walk out the next day.

Father, the saddest part is that I blamed you for the bad things that happened to me. I believed you let them happen because I was a bad person, and you didn't love me. But, the worst part of it all is that I didn't think I could trust you when it was me who couldn't be trusted all this time.

I know I'm not perfect, but I know, with your help, I can be better. I'm starting to understand that you don't expect me to be perfect either, but that you want me to be the best person I can be. Therefore, I need to be more concerned with making "spiritual progress" than achieving "spiritual perfection."

Can you ever forgive me, Father? Will you take my pride, resentments, anger, and rebellion from me and help me find peace and forgiveness? Will you help me to be honest with myself and others? I'm ready to change, Father. I'm ready to follow your teachings and give my life over to you. In Jesus Christ's name, I pray, amen.

CHAPTER 12

I wake up when the cabin lights come on and realize I'm still in a kneeling position on my bunk. My legs are cramped, and my back is stiff, but I don't know how much I slept.

I continued praying throughout the night. Each time another memory came into my mind that I needed to lay before God, I got back on my knees and asked for forgiveness. I can't tell you if it was many individual prayers or one or two long prayers, but since I couldn't sleep, I talked with God.

After breakfast, Pit Bull gives us our assignments at the corral. Drew and I are both working at the slaughterhouse today, but I'm not angry for some reason. It's just another day on the ranch for all of us.

Instead of cleaning up after the butchers, our job is to herd the cows and pigs that come in on semi-trucks into the queue. It bothers me that we have to use cattle prods to move them because they are so scared.

I'd hate to be one of these animals, just knowing I was about to die at the hands of a butcher. Fortunately, I quickly learn that some cows are so frightened that just the sound of the electricity arcing between the two posts is enough to get the cows moving. I've seen enough animals abused that I don't want to contribute to it in any way.

One truck is so overcrowded that the pigs are on top of one another. I have no idea how they got them in there, but several pigs are already dead—either trampled, suffocated, or scared to death, I don't know which.

I thought the sounds of a dying cow would never fade from my memory, but the squeals of a dying pig will haunt me forever. When I close my eyes at night, I can still hear their high-pitched screams echo off the walls in my head.

More than one pig is still very much alive when he is stuck in the neck with a double-edged blade. From what I witnessed, most pigs bleed out in less than a minute, but I witnessed several times when the pigs had to be stuck a second-time several minutes down the line.

The worst part of it all is that the full-time workers don't seem to care. One worker kicks a pig in the head when he tries to run in the wrong direction. Another is beaten with a club when he tries to escape the man with the penetrating captive bolt.

I'm just grateful there isn't a truckload of horses delivered because I don't think I could watch someone slaughter a horse. I enjoy spending time with the horses on the ranch, and I can't look at them without thinking of them as a friend.

I've never seriously considered becoming a vegetarian, but today convinced me that the slaughter of animals is unnecessarily cruel, no matter how "humanely" it's done. I'll never look at a plate of ribs, or a steak, the way I did before. On the way back to the ranch, I'm in the backseat while Drew rides up front with Pit Bull.

"I don't want to ever work there again," I say with solemn determination.

Pit Bull nearly comes out of his seat and lets loose on me about how little he cares about what I want and don't want. When we get back to the ranch, he starts yelling at me some more as I get out of the truck. Finally, it's my turn not to care, and I just ignore him and walk away.

That may not have been the wisest thing I've ever done, but I had to say something. I don't think prison diversion programs are supposed to be slave labor camps. It's no wonder Dr. Hartwell keeps us locked up in this place. The first chance I get, I'm going to the police. Maybe they'll do something about all the bull crap going on up here.

* * * * *

I'm eating dinner with Todd and Drew when Vincent comes over and sets his tray down across from me. I like Vince, he's pretty mellow, and he's got a dry sense of humor that reminds me of Nate.

"How are the tacos?" he asks, watching me take a bite of one and drip salsa down my shirt.

"Not bad," I reply, "but I'm not eating beef at the moment."

"You work at the slaughterhouse today?"

"Yup. I won't be eating any bacon in the morning, either."

"Cows and pigs, huh? How'd you manage to get on that detail?"

"Just lucky, I guess."

"Yeah," Vince says, "Once Pit Bull sicks his teeth into you, he doesn't let go, does he?"

"Yeah, well, I told him how I felt about it today."

"Oh really?" Vince says. "I'll bet he took that well."

I chuckle. "About as well as I expected. I'm sure I'll be on slaughterhouse duty every day for the foreseeable future."

"Did you know that eight billion land animals are slaughtered each year?" Todd asks at the first break in our conversation. "And that's just in the United States! If you include sea animals, it's over 55 billion."

Vincent knows Todd and that he has an unlimited supply of useless information. So, he changes the subject as quickly as possible.

"Hey Jake, I've got a question I've been meaning to ask you."

"Yeah? What is it?"

"Out of everyone here that I've talked to, you've had more experience with recovery than anyone else. So I was wondering if you have any advice you could give me."

Vince's question catches me off guard. I don't feel like I'm the best person to give advice about staying clean, but he did ask.

"The best advice I can give you, Vince, is that if you never want to drink again, you have to surrender to your disease."

"I've heard people say that before," he admits, "but I don't get it. What does that mean—'surrender to your disease?'"

I'm hesitant to share my observations because, well, as I said before, I've been in and out of drug treatment centers for the last six years. The longest period of sobriety I had in all that time was seven months, but I do know what worked for me and what didn't work.

"Surrendering to your disease means that you have to accept the fact that you are an alcoholic and that you will always be an alcoholic. Even if you stay sober for the next thirty years, you will still be an alcoholic—but you'll be a recovering alcoholic."

"That's it?" he asks with a look of disappointment on his face. "I just have to accept that I am now, and always will be, an alcoholic?"

"If you can do that," I tell him, "you will never have to take another drink as long as you live. I can promise you that."

He doesn't look like he believes me, so I try another tack.

"Have you ever heard the phrase, 'one is one too many, and a thousand is never enough?'"

"No," he says, "what does it mean?"

"It means that you can never say, 'Oh, I'll just have one drink' or ' one little bump.' It doesn't work that way. If you allow yourself to use just one time, no matter how much sobriety you have under your belt, you will be right back in the throes of addiction, just as if you'd never stopped drinking or using drugs in the first place."

"When I got clean for the first time, I walked out of that in-patient treatment center thinking—no, fully convinced—that I would never drink or use drugs again."

"What happened?"

"Within 6 months, I'd convinced myself that I was not an addict and that I'd be okay if I just had one beer. *One* beer!

After I drank that first beer, I couldn't stop drinking for two years. I went from beer to liquor in less than a week, and within two months, I started doing drugs all over again. One drink is one too many, and a thousand are never enough."

"So, what your saying is just never take that first drink?"

"Exactly. Surrendering to alcoholism (or drug addiction—it's the same) means accepting that you can never, ever take another drink. You have to get the idea that you might be able to drink like a normal person out of your head and keep it out at all costs. If you think about drinking, you're going to drink. So as soon as the thought of drinking enters your mind, replace it with another thought that is not about drugs or alcohol. Because if you don't, the beast inside of you will wake up and burn your house to the ground."

"The best way I've heard that tactic explained." Todd says, "is that you always have to 'think that next drink to the end.'"

"To the end of what?" Vince asks.

"To that inevitable end where alcoholics who drink always end up—powerless over alcohol again. One drink, and the compulsion for another will hit you like a speeding train. And that compulsion to drink will be with you every moment of every day until you die or accept that you can never drink again."

Vince shakes his head, trying to figure out another way. "But I'm 24 years old. It's not against the law to drink alcohol. I've got my entire life ahead of me. And you're telling me I can't ever drink again—not even when I'm old and retired and have nothing else to do all day. That just doesn't seem fair."

"You're right, it's not fair, but it's reality. So here's another way to look at it. Say you love guns, and you go out and get a gun and a concealed carry permit. There's nothing wrong with that, right?"

"Not that I know of," he says.

"What would happen if you went around shooting up the neighborhood? I'm not saying killing anyone, just firing a shot now and again, as the impulse suits you."

"The police would arrest me."

"Yes, and what else?"

"They'd take my gun away?"

"And what else?"

"They'd take my concealed carry permit away?"

"Why would they take all those things away from you. This is America, and the 2nd Amendment to the Consitution says you have the right to own a gun.

"Well, c'mon, if you abuse the right to have a gun, you're no longer fit to own one or carry one."

"Exactly."

"So, you're saying that because I abused alcohol, I've forfeited my right to ever drink again?"

"Yes, and for the same reason you'd never be able to legally own another gun. It's the same with any liberty—like driving a car. If you abuse that right and put others in danger, you're right to drive will be taken away from you."

Vince nods his head. "Huh. I guess I've never looked at it that way. I've lost my right to drink, haven't I?"

"It sounds like it to me. Is that something you can live with?"

"What other choice do I have?"

CHAPTER 13

"Hey," Erika says as she walks down the pier toward me in running shorts, a t-shirt, and a pair of trail-running shoes. "I'm going for a run. You wanna join me?"

"You're going for a run? Now? *Here?*"

"Sure, why not?"

"Because…hmmm." I realize I don't know why not. "I would, but I don't have any running shoes."

"What'd you wear getting here?"

"A pair of Chuck Taylors."

"Go get 'em."

"They don't have any shoelaces!"

"Just go get them and meet me up at the stables in 5 minutes," she says, breaking into a run up the hill. "If you don't want to go, I'm sure I can find someone else to go with me."

Two seconds later, I'm walking up the hill to the cabin shaking my head, thinking how manipulative women can be. Who wouldn't want to spend time with a beautiful girl? She could talk anyone into running a marathon. There's just something about a tall, long-legged girl in short running shorts that can be highly persuasive.

I'm changing into something more appropriate for running than a pair of jeans and a button-down shirt when Drew walks in.

"Where're you going?"

"Erika and I are going for a run

"In those? He asks, pointing to my Chuck Taylors.

"Yup, Erika says she's got a plan."

"Running in those shoes will destroy your feet. They have no arch support."

"You got anything better?" I ask, knowing he's right.

"Yeah, as a matter-of-fact, I do."

Drew walks over to his bunk and gets down on his hands and knees. "Here, try these on," he says, pulling out a pair of running shoes from under his bunk.

"I didn't know you were a runner.

"Yeah, well, I'm not much of a runner, but I bought them a long time ago in the case I did start running. They've been sitting in my closet for almost a year. So I figured I'd bring them with me in case I felt like running."

"Do you feel like running?"

"No," he laughs, "I ain't gonna be no third wheel. You take 'em. If you like 'em, keep 'em."

I've already slipped them on, sans shoelaces, of course, but they're a good fit. "You're not gonna use these?"

"No," Drew says, "Besides, if I need another pair, I'll get them back home."

"Wow! Thanks," I exclaim, "I'll give 'em a try."

"Okay. Tell Erika I said 'hello.'"

"I will," I say as I walk out into the cool evening air and feel a surge of excitement ripple through my body.

Erika's already waiting for me when I get to the barn with a handful of zip ties.

"Those don't look like any Chuck Taylors I've seen before."

"They're not. Drew just gave them to me. What are those zip ties for?"

"Shoelaces," she says, pointing down at her shoes. "There's a whole box of them on a shelf in the barn."

"That's a good idea," I say, admiring her resourcefulness. How do they work?"

"We're gonna find out," she says, handing me a half-dozen zip ties and taking one of the shoes from me.

The zip ties are smaller than regular size, and I have no idea what they are used for on a ranch, but then, in my experience, zip ties are good for just about anything. Erika shows me how she put them in her shoes, and I start working on the other shoe.

"There you go," she says after inserting the last couple without pulling them tight. "Depending on how tight you make them, you might have to replace the top two or three ties to get your shoes on and off."

I'm impressed. We just found another use for zip ties! Furthermore, I won't have to worry about them coming untied and tripping on them.

"You ready?" she asks.

I haven't run in a couple of years, I mean, not seriously. I've run from the cops several times, but you don't have to be that fast when you're running from a police officer who's 50-pounds overweight and has a Starbucks latte in one hand and a Krispy Kreme doughnut in the other.

"Ready as I'm gonna be," I reply, wondering how healthy my lungs might be after smoking for the last three years.

Erika starts down the road, and I try to keep up. I hope she's not planning to go more than three or four miles because I already feel winded. We end up following the dirt road that leads back to Highway 2 until it comes to an intersection with another dirt road that I've seen before but never taken.

"Follow me," Erika says and takes a left which puts the sun at our backs. It's so much easier to tell directions in Seattle, where all the mountains are to the East.

I can tell Erika is a good runner. Her head and upper body stay level as she runs, which means she doesn't bounce like many runners do. I used to run like that—believing that the more ground covered in each step resulted in a faster pace. But I know that's not true anymore. Gazelles and cheetahs run quite differently, and only one is the fastest land animal—the other is usually dinner.

Erika is 5 foot, 8 inches, and lean, yet she takes shorter steps than less experienced runners with shorter legs. She must have had an excellent running coach in high school who taught her that the key to running faster is not a lengthened stride but a quicker turnover rate.

"What's your optimal cadence?" I ask, referring to how many times each foot strikes the ground per minute.

"88-90," she says, "unless I'm running trails, then it's closer to 100."

"Seriously?" I ask. "I would have thought you would have a lower cadence on uneven terrain."

"Not if you're running competitively," she explains, "a higher cadence gives you greater stability, and that's the key to running fast on trails."

"Which do you prefer?" I ask, trying to keep her talking while we run.

"I love trails because you have to stay focused, and the scenery changes all the time. I can run for six or seven hours, and it feels like half that. Road races are tedious, and unless I really zone out, I get bored pretty quickly."

"What's the longest distance you've ever run?" I ask, trying not to gasp for air between every word.

"Fifty miles."

"*Fifty miles*? Are you insane?"

"No, lots of people run ultramarathons. There's a ton of races longer than 26.2 miles. In fact, I'm planning to run my first 100-miler next year."

My hopes of getting Erika to ease off the pace by getting her talking and winded isn't working. She's running like this is a leisurely pace for her. I, on the other hand, am trying to suck every last molecule of oxygen out of the air.

"You think we could slow it down a little?"

"Oh, yeah, sorry," she says. "It just feels so good to run again, doesn't it?"

"Yeah."

We've probably run a couple of miles, and I'm starting to wonder how far Erika intends to run. I'm getting thirsty, and I don't see any aid stations out here or convenience stores.

"How far are you planning to go?" I ask, trying not to sound too pathetic.

"Just a little further," she says. "There's a spot up here I want to show you."

"You've been out here before?"

"We rode out here on horseback one evening," she says, "there were some cows that wandered out here, and we had to drive them back to the ranch."

"Does all this land belong to the Hartwell's"

"All the way to the river," she says.

"What river?"

"The Columbia River," she says, slowing to a walk and taking a detour off the road.

We walk about 300 feet through scraggly bushes and sagebrush until we come to a cliff's edge that drops 85 feet to a slow-moving river.

"*No...freakin'...way...,*" I stammer as I stand ten feet back from the ledge. There is nothing between us and the river but empty space. "That river must be a quarter-mile wide."

"Isn't it amazing?" Erika asks, standing next to me, looking out over the flat plains of Eastern Washington.

We are standing on the rim of a canyon—more of a gorge, actually—where the Columbia River has cut a swath through the high-mountain plains of Central Washington. Except for a two-lane highway on both sides of the river, the landscape is devoid of human existence.

"I can't believe this is here," I tell Erika as I inch toward the edge to get a better view. "That must be a sheer rock face all the way down to the river."

"Jake, please, don't go any further," she says, willing to go no closer to the drop-off. "This is as close as we need to get. Unfortunately, as you can see, there aren't any fences here to keep us from falling over the side."

"Are you afraid of heights?"

"Terrified," she says, holding out a hand to entice me back away from the cliff.

I take her hand and step back away from the ledge, still drinking in the beauty of the vista before us. I feel her hand relax when I'm back at her side and realize I've never been this close to her alone. Then, before I even realize what is happening, she leans up and kisses me.

Her skin is as soft as a rose petal, and my heart flutters for a second or two as if it forgot how to beat. When her lips part, we engage in a kiss that I will measure all others by for the rest of my life. The entire world melts away as if we are the only two people on the planet.

When she opens her eyes, she giggles, gives me another kiss, and takes off running back the way we came. There is nothing I could possibly do at this moment but follow her.

The two miles going back fly by like cars on a train, and I forget how winded I felt on the way out. I just discovered a new level of happiness I didn't know existed. I wouldn't care if we never stopped running.

* * * * *

Erika and I both know it wouldn't be wise to be seen kissing around the cabins even though it's already dark, so we just say goodnight, and she heads toward Cabin 4. It's getting close to lights out anyway, and I need a shower before turning in. Maybe even a cold shower.

"What are you smiling about?" Drew asks as I walk in. His bags are packed and sitting by his bunk.

"Oh, man! I forgot you're leaving tomorrow. I should have stuck around here for your last night."

"No, don't sweat it," Drew says. "Besides, I don't think you're gonna miss *me* too much. You look like you just won the lottery."

"I think I did."

"Cool, man. I'm happy for you two. I was just hangin' with these homies," nodding toward Seth and Todd, who are both lying on their bunks.

"Yeah, Seth is going to Utah to work with Drew when he gets out of here," Todd informs me.

"What about Monica?" I ask.

"She's going with him," Todd explains as if Seth weren't even in the room.

"And are they still getting married?"

"I don't know. I'll have to ask him. Hey Seth, are you and Monica still getting married?"

"Dude, I'm *right here*," Seth injects, "and yes, we're still getting married. Probably down in Vegas."

"You think going to Las Vegas is good after coming out of rehab?" I ask.

"Yeah, man. I've got this thing. I'm never using again. That's why I'm going to Utah. They don't have drugs down there, or alcohol, or cigarettes. I'm gonna be a Mormon!"

"I don't know about all that," Drew says, "but I'll watch out for him. My uncle has a place they can stay, and the work's a lot like here. So it'll be a good place for them to start out."

"What about you, Todd? What are you planning to do when you leave?" I ask.

"Probably just go back to Portland," he says, a bit sullen.

"Why don't you come with us?" Drew asks. "There's a great community college there. You could work for my uncle during the day and take evening classes to get your GED. He's got plenty of room and needs the help."

"Don't they have an aviation program there?" Todd asks.

"I think so," Drew replies. "Why, do you want to fly planes?"

"Helicopters," Todd says. "My dad was a helicopter pilot in Vietnam. So I've always wanted to fly helicopters. I think he'd love it if we had that in common."

Just as I am about to ask what kind of flying he'd like to do, Pit Bull kicks our door in and almost knocks it off its hinges.

"Well, well, well, look what we have here, boys."

Pit Bull walks into our cabin, reeking of alcohol. The three prison guards that follow him are also drunk. Pit Bull walks over to where I'm standing and says, "Hi Jake!" The smell of alcohol is so strong I almost catch a buzz from his breath.

"Or should I call you Jacob?"

"Call me whatever you want," I reply, trying to diffuse the situation.

"I like Jacob. It's very proper," he says. But do you know what name I like best, Jacob?"

"I haven't a clue."

"'Jacob Robert Coleman,' as in Robert Coleman—one of the richest men in the country. Isn't that right, Jacob?"

I'm absolutely stunned that Pit Bull just blew the lid off the secret I've kept since I arrived. I look over at Drew, who appears to be in a state of shock, and reply, "Yes."

The look on Drew's face is not one of anger but, sadness. It is a look of betrayal.

"Your dad is the CEO of Coleman Pharmaceutical Laboratories?" He asks. "The company that makes Metaphix?"

"Yes," I repeat, unable to look him in the eyes.

"We've got ourselves a real celebrity here, boys. Jake's dad is a billionaire."

I'm still too stunned to think clearly, so I walk straight past Pit Bull and his posse and out the cabin door to get some fresh air.

"Hey, Jake," Pit Bull calls from the veranda. "When are you gonna invite us over for a pool party or something? I'd sure love to meet your parents and tell them how proud they should be of their hard-working son."

I spin around angrily, "What's it to you, Pit Bull? Why do you care who I am?"

Pit Bull nearly stumbles as he tries to walk down the front steps. He gets in my face and pokes me in the chest. "Because you think you're so much better than the rest of us," he slurs.

"You're drunk! I don't think I'm better than anyone else. Why do you say that?"

"Because you think we should bow down to you and kiss your feet, don't ya, Jake? Is that why Erika likes you—because you have money?"

'You don't know me." I assert, not willing to back down any longer. "And what Erika and I do is none of your business."

"Sure, it is Jake. I need to know what's happening around here, so why don't you tell me."

"Stay the hell away from Erika and me."

"Or what? What're you gonna do, Jake? Call Daddy Warbucks and tell him we're not being nice to you?"

"Get out of my face," I yell back at him.

Pit Bull and I are both ready to throw punches, but a couple of the prison guards get in between us and pull us apart. The prison guards each put an arm around Pit Bull and lead him off toward the lodge. I can still hear him shouting something about a silver spoon when I walk back inside to talk to Drew.

"Drew, I was going to tell you...."

"Don't bother," he says. "I don't want an apology from you. I hope Roy's family wins that lawsuit and takes every penny your family has."

As if to punctuate his last statement, the lights cut out, and the cabin plunges into darkness. I have no idea what to say to Drew. I should have been honest with him when he told me about his cousin, but I wasn't. I didn't want it to get in between our friendship, but it has anyway.

*****

Drew is already gone when the lights come on to wake us up. I wanted just a few minutes to explain why I hadn't said anything about my family, but he's nowhere to be found. Once again, I find myself cursing my last name.

I don't even listen to the assignments when the parole officer gives them out after breakfast. I'm already in the back of the truck, steeling my nerves for another day at the slaughterhouse.

"C'mon, Jake!" Seth yells. "You and I are on the castration crew! This is going to be awesome!"

"*What* crew?"

"Didn't you hear the parole officer? We're castrating steers today. C'mon! I've got dibs on the first one."

I guess I'm not working at the slaughterhouse today after all. Instead, I'm teamed up with probably the only guy I know who would enjoy emasculating a steer. I'm not sure which is worse.

"Have you ever done this before?" I ask.

"No."

"Then how do you know what to do?"

"One of the prison guards is going to show us. But, hey, if we get done before the branding, maybe we can give that a shot, too."

"Wouldn't that be awesome?" I mutter.

"We're also vaccinating them, but a couple of the girls are on that crew."

"What about Todd? What's he doing?" I ask as we walk toward the toolshed.

"He's taking a headcount of bulls and heifers."

I contemplate asking Pit Bull if I can just work at the slaughterhouse or switch with Todd, but I know if I show any weakness, he'll exploit it.

I follow Seth to the corrals. We pick up our gloves and an emasculating tool that looks something like a pair of steel plyers with crimping blades on the end. Neither of us has any idea what we're doing, and Seth can't wait to do it.

There are two prison guards on horseback, one tending a fire pit and another prepping a gigantic shot needle. The rest of us are standing around looking as clueless as a fencepost. Lucky for me, I don't see Pit Bull around, but I'm sure he'll show up soon and give me hell.

When the branding party starts, the two prison guards on horseback attempt to rope the closest calf, one by the head and the other by a back leg. Neither of them can get their lasso anywhere close to the calf, and they end up spooking the entire herd who run wildly about the corral.

Their next attempt is no better. The prison guards chase another calf and corner him while all the other calves run to the opposite end of the corral. One of the prison guards twirls his lasso overhead, only to have the hoop fall around him, roping himself and scaring his horse. The other prison guard is at least successful in throwing his lasso, but it misses the cow by 10 feet and catches on a fencepost. Finally, the calf realizes neither of the prison guards are threats and walks calmly between them to join the rest of the herd.

"That's enough," the Warden yells, storming out the back door of the lodge. "What the *hell* are you doing? You idiots ain't ready for ropin'! Whose stupid idea was this?"

The prison guards look at one another until someone finally cops to it, "It was my idea, Sue."

"Where's Pit Bull?"

"We ain't seen him this morning," another prison guard says. He told us to get things organized, and he'd be along shortly. So we just thought we'd get things started."

The Warden gets on her radio and calls for Pit Bull. When he doesn't come back over the radio, she curses some more and pulls the closest prison guard off his horse.

"Open that gate!" She yells, pointing to a gate along the edge of the corral. "Haven't you dimwits ever heard of a squeeze chute?"

Sue singles out a calf by steering her horse and herding the young bull toward the gate. When the calf passes through the gate, she tells the prison guard to close it, and the young bull finds himself in a long narrow chute leading to a separate pen.

Assuming he's now out of harm's way, the bull saunters through the chute toward the empty pen. Halfway through the chute, he enters a section that looks oddly different than the others. Before the calf realizes what is happening, Sue pulls a lever, and the sides of the chute squeeze in on the cow until it can't move.

"See how easy that was?" Sue says. "Now, get me a branding iron and some gloves."

With a branding iron in hand, its tip smoking and the color of gray ash, Sue walks over to the calf and presses the scorching brand to the bull's hide, rolling it from top to bottom for just a few seconds. Thick white smoke rises from the bull's hide, and he groans slightly, but not as much as I would expect. When the smoke clears, the bull's left flank bears the Serenity Ranch brand—a distinct "SR" inside of a diamond.

"Bring me them nut cutters," Sue says, looking at Seth, "and observe."

She takes the bull's scrotum and finds one of the spermatic cords, which runs from the testicles up into the steer's body. Once she has one of the cords, she puts the crimpling blades on either side and squeezes them tight while counting aloud to ten. Next, she moves the tool down about one centimeter and does it again.

Sue finds the other spermatic cord and repeats the process, thus crushing and cutting off the blood supply to the testicles, which will shrivel and die over the next few weeks. I squirm uncomfortably for each 10-second application, extremely grateful that I'm not in the squeeze chute. It's difficult to watch, but at least there isn't any blood, and the cow doesn't seem too concerned.

Finally, Sue takes the shot needle and pokes the cow in the neck. The syringe is six inches long and as thick as a watering hose. The grip looks like a caulking gun, and when squeezed, a plunger forces the serum into the needle and the newly minted bull.

The serum is a combination vaccine for tetanus, respiratory diseases, and blackleg. After what the bull has already been through, it proves to be the least traumatic thing that's happened in the last two minutes. Once injected, Sue pulls the lever, and the cow scurries out of the chute into the holding pen.

"Any question?" she asks, handing the syringe back to the nearest prison guard. "Then get to work!"

CHAPTER 14

By now, everyone at the ranch knows who I am. Drew is gone. Erika is working at the slaughterhouse, and I'm making sure 1-year old bulls never reproduce. Even Seth and Todd seem to be aloof, or maybe they're just really into castration.

By the time we finish, it's lunchtime, and I eat alone at a separate table. I can hear people whispering about me, and I am not in the mood for conversation.

After lunch, Pit Bull shows up and checks the brands to make sure everything went okay. Unfortunately for him, it looks like he's had a miserable morning. He must have a severe hangover from the previous night.

He gives out assignments for the afternoon. So it looks like I'll be in the chicken coop shoveling poop for the rest of the day. I hate the smell of chicken coops, but I'm happy to be working alone. It's a relief not having to answer the types of questions I've been getting all morning.

One inmate approached me with a sales pitch about using drones in the livestock industry. Seems there are many tasks a drone could do better and faster than a rider on horseback.

"That's interesting," I say, "but why are you telling me this?"

"I'm looking for a partner, you know, someone who can cover the startup costs and help me get this going."

"Dude, I'm an addict, just like you. I don't have a bunch of money lying around to invest in a new business idea."

He gets pissed, calls me a liar, and walks away. It's interesting how people change when they think you have money.

Another guy tells me he's got a cousin who works at a casino in Jackpot, Nevada. If we went in together, we could make a killing at the tables with the help of his friend. I'm flabbergasted.

It's better that I just work alone in the chicken coop. If you're careful, less dust and dirt gets in the air, and that makes it easy to breathe—or I should say "easier" to breathe, because the smell of a ripe chicken coop is rediculous. Luckily, I have a balaclava I can pull over my head to keep some of the dust out of my mouth, nose, and ears.

After dinner, Todd, Seth, and I saddle the horses and ride out to reroute some of the irrigation ditches. We don't talk much, but I think everything will be fine after everyone gets over who I am.

When we get back to the corrals, we tend to the horses and get ready to call it a day when Erika shows up at the barn. I can tell she's upset by the look on her face. She must have had a rough day at the slaughterhouse.

The first words out of her mouth are, "I need to talk to you."

"Okay, are you going to shower first, or are we going on a run?"

"We're running. Now!" she says.

"Okay, let me get changed, and I'll meet you down by the pier."

"Hurry," she says. "It's important."

I change into some running clothes and slip on the shoes Drew left me. Fortunately, they are loose enough to get my foot in and out without cutting the zip ties.

It's absolute insanity that we're not allowed to have shoelaces in our shoes when we're working with all kinds of ropes, shears, leather straps, and sharp tools all day long. But then again, you come to terms with crazy when you check into rehab.

It's a beautiful evening for a run—the time of year when the sun hangs on the horizon, bathing the mountains and valleys with its last rays of the day. I'm staring at the reflection of the mountains on the lake when Erika walks up behind me.

"Hey," I say, expecting her warm smile and maybe a little kiss. But when I turn around, she isn't smiling. In fact, she looks downright scared.

"C'mon, we've got to run, Jake," she says, turning toward the road and leaving me in the dust.

I have to sprint to catch up to her, and when I do, I ask, "Is this about what Pit Bull said last night? About my father?"

"No," Erika says as she settles into a pace much faster than I'd like. "I don't care who your father is. It's about Pit Bull and *me*."

I stop in mid-stride and ask, "You and Pit Bull?"

Erika keeps running and yells over her shoulder, "It's not like that. I'll explain in a few minutes."

I'm chasing her again, but it takes twice as long to catch up to her this time. "Can you slow down a little?"

"No, Jake. It's not safe here anymore."

"What do you mean it's not safe here?"

Erika ignores my questions and keeps pushing the pace down the same road we followed last evening. When we reach the intersection, we take the left turn and run over a slight rise before she slows to a walk.

I'm still catching my breath when she looks at me and says, "I know who you are, Jake, and I don't care. If I were in your shoes, I'd have kept it quiet too. It's nobody's business here who your family is."

I'm shocked. If I expected anyone to be mad that I hadn't been more forthcoming about my personal life, I thought it would be Erika.

"I haven't been entirely honest with you either," she says and stops in the middle of the road.

"What do you mean?"

"Jake, I'm an undercover reporter for the *Los Angeles Times*. I'm here on assignment to write an exposé on the corruption inside prison deferment programs. I'm writing a piece about Serenity Ranch."

"This place is breaking all kinds of laws. I'm also pretty sure there's some serious corruption involving judges who send drug addicts here for treatment."

I can't help but shake my head, trying to make sense of what I just heard. "You're a reporter?"

"Yes," she says. "I wanted to tell you last night, but I was afraid you'd be angry with me."

"Why would I be angry with you?"

"Because I didn't mean for this to become so personal."

"You mean, you and me?"

"Yes. I didn't mean to fall in love with you."

I can tell she's terrified, so I take her in my arms and hold her close. "There's nothing to be scared of," I reply, "I have the same feelings for you."

"Yes, there is," Erika replies, pushing away from me enough to look me in the eyes. "I think Pit Bull knows who I am and is going to come after me."

"What are you talking about?"

"I was at the slaughterhouse today and found something that didn't make sense."

"What'd you find?"

"Cowhides with the Serenity Ranch brand on them."

"That's impossible," I say, "these cattle are sold at auction down in Oregon. There's no way they'd end up back here."

"That's what I thought, but there were six cows butchered today with the Serenity Ranch brand. I saw them with my own eyes at the tannery."

"But none of the cows from here have been sold, right?"

"None have been *sold* that I know of, but quite a few cows have disappeared."

"You mean stolen?"

"Yes, remember telling me about the tire marks from a trailer that day we had that massive storm, and the power was out? The prison guard said he would tell Pit Bull about the tire tracks and the cut wire and that Pit Bull would tell the Warden so she could file a police report."

"Yeah, so?" I ask.

"Did you ever see a sheriff or police car come up here to investigate?"

"No, but that doesn't mean they didn't."

"True, but maybe they didn't because no one filed a report."

"Why wouldn't Sue file a police report. It was probably that Goodman guy. He's been trying to get this property for a long time, right?"

"What if it wasn't Goodman? What if that's just a decoy? What if it were someone on the inside?"

"On the inside? You mean like one of the prison guards?"

"No. I mean, like *Pit Bull!*" Erika shouts, "He's got a truck, and I'm sure he has access to a trailer, right? So maybe he's the one rustlin' the cattle and selling them to his buddy Shane."

"But why would he do that?" I ask. "If this ranch goes under, he's out of a job."

"You're right." Erika nods, "but guess who inherits the revenue from this property if Dr. Hartwell dies and the bank calls in the loan?"

It takes me a minute, but then it comes to me like a flash of lightning. "*Vanessa!*"

"Exactly. And guess who Pit Bull had in the truck with him today when he picked me up at the slaughterhouse?

"Vanessa?"

"Yup. I've always suspected something was going on between them," she says. "I've seen them together too many times to be a coincidence. I even saw them kissing one time, but they didn't know anyone was around."

"Okay, so what are you saying? If Dr. Hartwell dies, Sue has to sell the ranch, and Vanessa gets nothing. How does Vanessa get anything out of it if Sue's family owned the land in the first place?"

"Think about it, Jake. Once Dr. Hartwell is gone, the bank will foreclose on the loan unless Sue can pay it off—which we know she can't. So once the ranch is sold, the only thing standing between Vanessa and her inheritance is Sue.

"You think Vanessa would kill her stepmother?"

"I don't know about Vanessa," she says, "but I have no doubt Pit Bull could make her death look like an accident."

"Oh my gosh. You're right. But how does that put you in danger?"

Erika shakes her head and sighs. "Because I asked too many questions on the ride back to the ranch today? I hadn't put all the pieces together about Vanessa and Pit Bull, and I asked Pit Bull about the cowhides I found at the tannery. I was sitting in the backseat, and from the looks they gave each other, they know I'm on to them."

"Holy crap. But they didn't say anything? They just dropped you off at the lodge, and that was it?"

"I think I surprised them enough that they panicked and didn't know what to do. It got super quiet after that, and no one said anything until we got back. Pit Bull and Vanessa don't know who else knows what's going on, so they've got to figure that out before they do anything."

"What do we do now?" I ask, still trying to wrap my mind around everything I've just learned.

"First of all, I've got to hide this," she says, pulling a small notebook from under her shirt.

I've seen Erika with this notebook in the evenings, but I'd always just figured it was her journal. It's small, about six inches, by nine inches, and about an inch thick. It's double-wrapped in two Ziplock bags.

"What's that?"

"All the notes I've taken over the last four months. I've documented everything from the number of patients that come through here to the forced labor at the slaughterhouse and all the things I've seen and heard that implicate the Hartwells in money laundering, bribery, and the violation of labor laws."

"What labor laws?"

"The ones that make it illegal to force people to work at a slaughterhouse without receiving minimum wages and overtime pay. Laws that require treatment facilities to be licensed by the state. Laws protecting people from being locked inside their living quarters at night, or behind barbed-wire fences to keep them from leaving."

"You've been documenting all this?"

"All that and more, Jake."

"There's more?"

"I'm fairly sure there're a few judges out there who get a cut of the money to send addicts here to work as free labor."

"What money?"

"This place is billed as a drug and alcohol treatment center, and someone, whether it's the family or an insurance company, pays about $75,000 for six months of treatment."

"What treatment?"

"Exactly!" Erika replies. "Who knows where all that money is going either. I'm pretty sure it's being used to pay off some judges. Also, unless you haven't noticed, quite a few people are driving around in shiny new trucks."

"What about Pit Bull?"

"He's an accomplice to all of this and probably the most dangerous of them all."

"What's with the Ziplock bags?"

"I've been hiding this journal in the water tank on the back of the toilet in our cabin. If someone knew what's written in here or what I'm doing here, I could be in a lot of danger."

"So, what are we gonna do with that journal?" I ask.

"I don't know," she says, "but I've got to keep it safe. Maybe we can take it out and bury it somewhere until we figure out a plan."

"What about hiding it under a rock or something?"

"As long as it stays dry and out of Pit Bull's and The Warden's hands, I don't care where we put it."

"What about hiding it in the barn back at the ranch?"

"That's too close," she says, just as we hear the rumbling of a truck over the hill.

"Oh no! They're coming, Jake. Run!"

"No way," I say, "Pit Bull isn't that stupid."

Just as the words leave my mouth, I spot Pit Bull's truck speeding down the road about a half-mile behind us.

"Oh, crap! Run, Erika!"

We both run as fast as we can away from the ranch, hoping we haven't been spotted. But, when we see the truck again, it's less than a quarter-mile behind us, and there's no doubt they're after us.

"Run to the cliff!" Erika shouts as we approach the area where we left the road the other night.

I follow her off the road toward the canyon ledge where we kissed the time before. I hear the truck plow through the sagebrush behind us and slam on the brakes just as we get to the edge and stop. A dust cloud blinds us as both truck doors open, and Pit Bull and The Warden step out.

"Give me the book," I whisper to Erika as the dust cloud hangs between us and the truck. Erika hands me the book, and I shove it in the back waistband of my shorts.

When the dust clears, Erika and I are standing just a few feet from the ledge, and Sue and Pit Bull are leaning against the truck, laughing.

"Oh, isn't this sweet!" The Warden says.

Pit Bull joins in, singing, "Two little lovebirds sitting in a tree."

"You know," Sue says, looking at Erika, "I really liked you in the beginning. You were tough, worked hard, and didn't take *shit* from anyone. You reminded me of me when I grew up on this ranch."

"But you, Jake," she continues. "you're the one who surprised me. Who knew you'd turn out to be Robert Coleman's son?"

"Let's just shoot 'em now," Pit Bull says, pulling the same gun from its holster with which he'd shot Shasta.

"Hold on," The Warden says, "I want to ask Jake here some questions. It ain't every day we get such a prominent visitor here at the ranch. How is your dad, anyway, Jake?"

"What do you care?"

"Because I haven't seen him in over thirty years,"

"Wait. You know my father?"

"I sure do. We went to school together over on the west side. We were great friends until your dad met your mom. She didn't like me much when she found out that Bob and I had a history."

"You dated my father?"

"For over a year," Sue says. "I thought we would get married, but then Bob met your mother over the summer, and she had more to offer."

"You mean she had *money*?" I ask, remembering how my father resented his father-in-law's involvement in the early days of their marriage.

"Oh, she came from money, all right, and your father saw that as a way to get what he wanted most."

"A degree from Yale?"

"Not just a degree from Yale, but a degree in biochemistry, from one of the leading universities in the field. In the end, he chose her over me."

"Is that how I got here? You and my father worked this out with Judge Chamberlain?"

Sue laughs. "No, Chamberlain has nothing to do with your father, but he and I do have an arrangement that helps each other when he sends me addicts from his jurisdiction here."

"You mean *kickbacks*," Erika says.

"I think of them as 'finder's fees,' not kickbacks. Sending addicts to prison does nothing to rehabilitate them. Developing a work ethic is the only way to rehabilitate an addict, right Pit Bull?"

"Yes, ma'am," he says, ready to get on with the action.

"Even Pit Bull here was an addict at one time," The Warden continues, "came here barely able to wipe his own ass. Isn't that right, Pit Bull?"

Pit Bull doesn't answer.

"Is that why he's rustling cattle from the ranch?" I ask.

"What are you talking about?" The Warden asks, completely caught off-guard.

"He's stealing cattle right from under your nose and selling them to the slaughterhouse. Ain't that right, Pit Bull?"

"I am not! He's lying. I ain't got nothin' to do with that!"

Sue turns on Pit Bull as anger floods her face. "Is that true? Do you have something to do with the missing cattle?"

Erika sees what's happening and steps in. "It's true! I saw the hides with the Serenity Ranch brand this afternoon at the slaughterhouse. I even asked Pit Bull and Vanessa about it on the way back to the ranch,"

"*Vanessa?* Is Vanessa involved in this?" The Warden demands, staring at Pit Bull.

Suddenly, Pit Bull swings the gun around and shoots the Warden in the chest. She drops to the ground with a scream still in her throat.

"Now, see what you made me do?" Pit Bull exclaims, pointing the gun back at Erika and me. "Now I'm going to have to make this look like you shot her. That won't be so hard," he says, putting the gun back in his holster and pulling a hunting knife from a sheath on the other side of his belt. "Just gotta make it looks like she attacked you after finding out you're the son of the billionaire that left her for another woman."

"Nobody's gonna believe that," I shout, taking Erika by the hand and stepping back another foot away from Pit Bull.

"They will when I put your prints on the gun and her prints on this knife. It'll look like she found out who you were, brought you out here, and tried to kill you to take revenge on your father."

"What are you gonna do with her?" I ask, nodding to Erika, who tucks in behind me.

"Guess I'll have to shoot her too."

I look at Erika, and she looks at me. We both know what we must do. Before Pit Bull can close the distance between us, Erika and I turn, take two steps, and jump off the cliff, still holding hands.

CHAPTER 15

Since Nate drowned in the Yakima River, I have had an elemental fear of waters—particularly rivers. Swimming pools are no problem—I do fine if I can see the bottom and the water isn't moving. Oceans and lakes, however, have no appeal to me. I enjoy them immensely from the shoreline, but you won't find me frolicking in the surf or on a stand-up paddleboard.

Rivers are an entirely different story. I hate rivers. For years, I've had nightmares of drowning in a river, and I wake up in a panic, holding my breath and bathed in a puddle of sweat.

Sometimes, I am alone in my nightmares, while other times, there are people I know—a friend, a relative, someone I talked to on the street. They are always trying to help me get out of the river, but we can never hold on to one another.

I don't know why certain people show up in these nightmares. For example, one night, I dreamt that my second-grade teacher was trying to get me into a rowboat, but he couldn't get close enough for me to reach him. I know he was a good teacher, and I liked being in his class, but I have no idea why he showed up in my dream.

The worst nightmare I remember having was falling in a river and discovering ice on the surface that I couldn't break through. I can still feel the freezing waters and the dull thumping sounds I made trying to break through the ice. That nightmare felt like it went on for days, never-ending, just holding my breath until everything went black.

When I woke from that nightmare, I gasped for air so loudly that I woke my parents in the next room. My mother came in to check on me, but it was my father I needed, not her.

Erika and I fall for what feels like hours. It's interesting how the mind can slow down the passage of time in moments like this. Suddenly, I am aware of everything going on around me—my legs kicking involuntarily; Erika falling to my right and screaming unmercifully at the greenish-brown water below; the glint of sun reflecting from a shiny black truck passing by on the two-lane highway across the river; the smell of smoke in the air from a fire burning somewhere up-canyon.

Interestingly, I am not aware of how Erika's journal goes from the waistband of my shorts to my left hand. Grabbing hold of the book from behind my back is the one thing I do, of which I have no consciousness or memory.

When we splash into the water, it sounds like dynamite exploding beneath our feet, and then silence. I must close my eyes at some point during the fall. I don't remember the exact moment of impact; however, I do remember thinking that I need to keep my feet together or I'm going to have the world's worst 'wedgie.' After that, I remember nothing.

*****

When I open my eyes, the first thing I see is a beautiful, blonde-haired woman who looks at me like she just saw a ghost. The look of surprise on her face surprises me, and I glance about frantically, trying to understand where I am and recognizing absolutely nothing. But then I hear a voice I recognize, and all my fears fade away.

The voice is like that of a bird singing on a bright, sunny morning. It's a melody I love, although I don't know the words.

"Jake? Are you awake?"

"E-E-Erika?"

My mouth is dry, and her name tumbles out as if it were something I could no longer contain. But the face I see isn't Erika's—it's a man's face with glasses and several days' growth on his chin.

"Mr. Coleman, do you know where you are?"

"No," I reply, only certain that I am indoors and that someone should turn out the lights.

"You're at the University of Washington Medical Center," the doctor says, turning off the penlight he used to look at my pupils. "Do you know where that is?"

I become aware of my surroundings as my mind starts to clear. I can tell that I am lying in a hospital bed, with my left leg and arm suspended in the air.

I try to turn my head to the side, but I can't. It feels like my entire body is being restrained, but then I feel someone take my right hand in theirs and see Erika standing next to me out of the corner of my eye.

"Erika!"

"I'm here, Jake. I'm right here." Her voice is the most beautiful sound I've ever heard, and just seeing her beautiful face calms me in a way I will never understand. A tear runs down her cheek, but she is smiling and happy.

"I'm in the hospital," I reply, still trying to understand why my left arm and leg are in the air.

"That's right, Mr. Coleman. I'm Doctor Brown, head of the intensive care unit, and we've been taking good care of you. Do you remember how you got here?"

My memory starts flickering, and I see huge rotor blades spinning above me and lights flashing in my eyes. "A helicopter?"

"Good, Mr. Coleman. I'm glad to hear that you have some of your memories intact. You probably won't remember everything exactly as it happened, but we hope that bits and pieces come back over time. From what we've seen so far, it appears that your neurological condition is stable."

I haven't taken my eyes off of Erika the entire time Dr. Brown has been talking, and to be honest, I really haven't been listening.

"Are you okay?"

"I'm great!" Erika replies as she kisses my forehead. "I'm just so relieved that you're awake."

"How long have I been here?"

Erika looks at Dr. Brown and asks, "Two weeks?"

"Sixteen days," he replies, confirming the date with my medical charts.

"*Sixteen days?* What about you? Did you get hurt?"

"I sprained my ankle and strained some muscles in my back, but there's hardly a scratch on me. You're the one everyone's worried about."

I feel something metal pressing against the heel of my left foot.

"Can you feel this, Mr. Coleman?" Dr. Brown asks.

"Yes."

"How about this?" He says, checking for sensations in my toes and fingers.

"Yes. I feel that too."

"Any numbness or tingling."

"No. It just feels like you're stabbing me with a pair of scissors."

"It's just a writing pen, Mr. Coleman. Your nerves are a bit sensitive right now, but that's a good sign. I'm hopeful that your neurological pathways are working correctly and that there's no paralysis. So far, everything looks good."

"Why can't I move my neck?"

You broke your left leg and your left arm when you impacted the water," Dr. Brown explains. "You also cracked two vertebrae in your neck and had a severe concussion, but you were lucky not to have damaged any internal organs."

"I don't think it was luck," I reply, saying a quick prayer in my head.

"We put a rod in your femur to help the bones fuse and a pin in your elbow. The breaks in your cervical vertebrae are only fractures, so we didn't have to operate. If either one of them had broken, you'd likely be paralyzed from the neck down."

"Will I be able to run again?"

"*Run?*" Dr. Brown asks. "Let's get you standing first, and then walking, but as young and healthy as you are, and with a great physical therapy program, well, I don't see why not."

"Good," I reply, still looking at Erika. "Because I've got a pretty amazing running partner here who's going to help me train for my next marathon."

* * * * *

"Chelan County authorities are charging Duane Hatch, aka 'Pit Bull,' with first-degree murder in the death of Susan Hartwell. Hatch is expected to enter a not guilty plea, his attorney has stated, and that Hatch acted in self-defense."

"Authorities are still searching for Vanessa Hartwell, who is wanted on conspiracy to commit murder in the attempt to take the lives of Jacob Coleman, son of billionaire Robert Coleman, and the *L.A. Times* reporter, Erika Stevens. Anyone with information about her whereabouts should report it to the FBI Hotline at 800-CALL-FBI (800-225-5324)."

Erika puts the copy of the *Los Angeles Times* aside and looks at me. She's waiting for my reaction to her article.

"Well?" she says after several seconds go by, "are you going to say anything?"

"That was incredible. That article is the next Pulitzer Prize winner for sure."

"You really think so?" she asks, not always sure when I'm serious.

"Erika, your story made the front page of the *Los Angeles Times*! That should tell you how good it is. For me, it was the best article

I've ever read or had read to me, especially because I was part of it and still didn't know half that stuff was going on."

"You mean about Dr. Hartwell?" she asks.

"Yeah, I mean, how did you find out he died and was buried over a year ago, and they just wanted people to believe he was still alive?"

"I got suspicious when none of us had ever seen him. Then, once you told me about their financial problems, I snuck into the lodge one morning and discovered that there was no Dr. Hartwell. I checked every room in the house, and he wasn't there."

"That was also when I discovered Vanessa's and Pit Bull's relationship. I saw them kissing on the sofa, but I didn't know she was involved in the cattle rustling until I asked Pit Bull about the cowhides I found."

"Wow! And now the state is investigating the judges who've sent addicts to the ranch?"

"Yes," Erika replies. "Every one of them is being investigated for taking bribes and money laundering, and maybe other crimes we don't yet know about. We'll have to wait and see what the investigation uncovers. Who knew what? What money changed hands? Whether Serenity Ranch is guilty of violating labor laws.

We know they didn't pay their 'employees' any wages, let alone minimum wage, overtime pay, or other compensation, especially since every one of us had to pay to be part of their program, which should have covered room and board."

"Well, as I wrote in the article, most families thought their loved ones were getting treatment for drug and alcohol addictions, and we didn't see any of that. So it'll be interesting to see if the ranch gets sued in civil court for misrepresentation of services because not everyone was court-ordered to be there."

"Oh, yeah," I reply, "I forgot about that. Hey, have you heard anything from Drew?"

"No," Erika says, "I haven't had a chance to contact him."

There's a knock at the door, and I figure a nurse is coming in to take my vitals. Both Erika and I get a surprise when we see who it is.

"Anyone for a game of UNO?" Todd asks as he pushes the door open.

"Todd!" Erika and I shout together as he enters the room.

"How are you, buddy?" He asks, looking at my arm and leg in casts.

"I'm okay, Todd. How are you?" He comes over to my bed and gives me a big bear hug. "Careful," I say, "I don't want to be in here any longer than I have to be."

"Sorry, Jake," Todd says as he releases me. "We've been so worried about you since we heard what happened."

"We?" Erika asks, "Who else knows about us?"

"Everyone," Todd exclaims, with a big smile on his face. "We didn't know what happened to you until the FBI raided the ranch two days after you disappeared. By then, Pit Bull had disappeared, but they found him hiding in the woods up near the Canadian border a few days later."

"Yeah, we heard about that," Erika says. "He got busted trying to use his credit card."

"Any news about Vanessa?" I ask.

"Not yet." Todd says, "but did you know that Washington State has 22 million acres of forested area and only 11,000 law enforcement officers? So, if every police officer, border patrol agent, customs officer, probation officer, game warden, corrections officer, and campus public safety officers in the state were looking for her, each person would have to search 2,000 acres—and that's only in the woods. If you add the cities and non-forested areas…."

"Todd," I interrupt, "we get it—she could be anywhere."

"Oh, yeah, sorry," he replies. "That's what I meant."

"We know," Erika says, giving him a big hug, "it's good to see you, Todd."

"Have you heard anything from Drew?" I ask.

"He's here!" Todd replies.

"What do you mean, 'he's here?' Where is he?"

"He's outside in the waiting area. He wanted to come in but, well, he was afraid that you wouldn't want to see him, Jake. He's apprehensive about how you two left things."

"He's here?" Erika shouts, her eyes as big as mine.

"Go get him!" I yell, adding, "tell him to get his butt in here," as Todd races down the hallway.

Moments later, the door opens, and Drew walks in with a smile.

"Are you accepting visitors?" he asks, not entirely sure he should believe what Todd told him.

"Drew!" I yell, tears springing to my eyes. "Get over here."

Drew and I hug for a long time. I can feel his tears on the side of my face, and I know exactly how he feels. I thought I'd lost one of my best friends.

He looks at me—half of me in a cast, the other half hooked up to IV drips, heart monitors, and blood oxygen meters. "I can't leave you alone for a minute, can I, Jake?"

"Nope," I reply. "You leave, and two days later, this happens to me. I'm a mess!"

"Well, it's better than the alternative," he says, wiping more tears from his eyes."

"What do you mean?"

"I didn't get a chance to tell him yet," Erika says, her usual cheeriness missing from her voice.

"Tell me what?"

"Seth relapsed and overdosed on heroin a week ago."

"*What?*"

"When everyone got away from the ranch, Seth and Monica headed down to Las Vegas to get married."

"Yeah? So?"

"He and Monica got into a fight about something, and she ditched him. Left him and went back home."

"No one really knows what happened after that, but he was found dead in his hotel room a couple of days later with a needle in his arm."

"Seth is *dead?*" I ask, unable to believe what I've just heard.

"He was going to come work with me at my uncle's ranch, you know? I had everything lined up for him. His sister contacted me right after they found him."

"That sucks!" I reply, suddenly angry at the world over something with which I have no control.

"It's drugs, man," Todd adds. "There is no cure for addiction. None of us are immune to them—no matter how good we feel or how much time passes. We'll always be one 'bump' away from full-on addiction."

"It's true," I sigh, thinking back to my own relapses. "One is one too many, and a thousand never enough.'"

* * * * *

Erika and Todd go out to get us some real food. I'm already tired of this hospital garbage. This gives Drew and me a few minutes to talk.

"Drew, I just want to apologize for what happened between us at the ranch."

"No," Drew responds. "I'm the one who needs to apologize. You didn't do anything wrong. I shouldn't have reacted the way I did, and it's been eating me up inside."

"Well, I wish I'd have told you the truth when you told me about your cousin."

"You didn't have anything to do with his death," Drew replies. "I was still angry and sad and didn't know how to deal with it. I've had some time to reflect on it, and I have to let go."

"Let go…and let God?"

"Exactly."

"Speaking of God," I say as I reach my good arm toward the nightstand next to my hospital bed. "I've been reading The Book of the Mormons you gave me."

"*The Book of Mormon?*" He asks, laughing at me for still getting the name wrong.

"Yeah. I had no idea Mormons believe in Jesus Christ. I thought everyone prayed to Joseph Smith."

"It's a common misperception," Drew says, "and one that couldn't be further from the truth. We believe that Joseph Smith was a prophet, called by God, to bring forth The Book of Mormon, a history of God's dealings with people on the American continent. Like the Bible, it's a history of His dealings with the Jews and people in that part of the world."

"So, you don't worship Joseph Smith?"

"No. We don't worship Joseph Smith," he says. "We worship God the Eternal Father, and His son, Jesus Christ, period. But we do respect and admire the work Joseph Smith did to help restore many gospel truths that were lost from the earth after Christ was crucified and his apostles were killed."

"Okay, well, I'm still reading, but it has definitely given me a better understanding of how much God loves us. I mean, I always knew He gave His only begotten son, Jesus Christ, to die for us, but I never really understood how personal His sacrifice was to each of us."

"It makes it easier to believe He can restore us to sanity when we realize how much He's done for us, doesn't it?"

Yes…and it's way easier than believing in a tree."

* * * * *

When Todd and Erika get back, we eat two New York-style pepperoni and olive pizzas from a superb take-out place down the block. I'm sure I'll get an earful from the medical staff when they find out what my friends smuggled in, but when you've had a near-death experience like I just had, stuff like that doesn't matter.

Drew and Todd take off a little later because Drew has a flight to catch back to Salt Lake City. The FBI flew him up to their Seattle field office and interviewed him, Todd, and several other inmates about the Hartmans and Serenity Ranch. My doctor said I need another two days of recovery before they can interview me.

Erika has been at my side every day since we escaped from Serenity Ranch. How she survived without a scratch is beyond all comprehension. We've had a couple of conversations about what happened after we jumped into the river, and the only way either of us can comprehend it is to call it a miracle.

The fact that Erika and I both knew what we had to do that day on the cliff above the Columbia River mystifies us both. I have been deathly afraid of rivers since the last time I nearly drowned. To be completely honest, I've never set foot in a river since the day Nate died—not to float, not to fish, not to cool off in the blazing summer heat. I hate rivers!

Erika was no more inclined to jump than me. In fact, overcoming her fear of heights just to make the jump was unbelievable. County deputies measured the distance we fell at 85 feet. That's nearly the length of an NBA basketball court. As a result, neither of us can comprehend how we committed ourselves to jump, except that we knew we were already committed to one another.

When we told Todd that, he did some quick calculations in his head and told us that if the cliff was 85 feet high, we fell for 3 seconds and hit the water at speeds between 53 and 62 miles per hour. No wonder half my body is in a cast.

There were only two eyewitnesses—the guy driving the black truck and Pit Bull. Eddie Greely, the guy in the truck, says that he was driving South from Chelan to Wenatchee and watched us from the moment we jumped from the ledge to the second we hit the water. He said that, initially, he didn't believe either of us survived.

According to the 9-1-1 call, two people jumped from a cliff into the Columbia River and barely cleared the bank by more than a dozen feet. I hit the water first, somewhat at an angle, and Erika hit just after me, completely vertical. That was the difference between her physical condition after the fall and mine.

Mr. Greely later reported that we both surfaced immediately after but that only Erika was conscious. She dragged me to shore. By that time, Mr. Greely said another driver on Highway 97, the two-lane road next to the cliff, saw a young lady crawling up the grassy bank and pulling someone out of the river. We survived with his help, the ambulance, and the Life-Flight Aeromedical helicopter, although I was unconscious for 16 days.

The doctors kept Erika in the hospital for 48 hours for observation while they performed two surgeries on me. Then, when they released her, she came to my room and has been here ever since. They even brought in a separate hospital bed for her to sleep here, which has been great because there's not much room in my hospital bed, and there's no way she's sleeping in a hotel.

She started writing the article for the newspaper the day after our escape. It was a headline on the front page, although most of the article got buried under a story about the woes of Wall Street and how Nike's stock took a hit for accusations of using overseas child labor again.

If Erika hadn't written that article, Todd, Seth, Vincent, and everyone else would still be locked up on the ranch. It took her calling out corrupt judges from several states to invoke an investigation by federal authorities.

We all owe Erika an enormous debt, but no one as much as I. If it weren't for her, my body would be on the bottom of the Columbia River or already washed out to sea.

What neither of us can understand is how I held onto Erika's journal through the entire ordeal. One of the many miracles of that day was that I was still clutching her journal in my hand when we surfaced. Had it been in my waistband, it would have been lost on impact. Had it been in Erika's hand, she might not have been able to rescue me and get us both to shore. Had it not been double wrapped in plastic, it would never have survived the river.

Erika said that even though I was unconscious, she had to pry the book out of my hand. How is that even possible? How was any of this even possible? But I guess it will serve as another brick in the house of faith I'm building. With God, all things are possible.

CHAPTER 16

It's after 10:00 PM when I hear the knock on the door. Erika is writing a follow-up story to the article in the *Los Angeles Times* because they just found Vanessa. She hid in a hunting cabin on Mr. Goodman's property that only gets used in late-fall during deer season. Mr. Goodman kept the cabin stocked, and the cabin has its own well.

The funny thing is, a search helicopter spotted smoke coming from the chimney; otherwise, they wouldn't have found her. I guess nobody told her that lighting a fire in the fireplace puts smoke in the air—especially if you feed the fire freshly cut wood. I didn't think Vanessa was very bright—easy to look at, yes—but not very bright.

We both hear a knock, and Erika gets up and goes to the door. I have no idea who it could be, especially when I hear Erika ask, "Does he know you?" It's past visiting hours, and nurses and doctors may knock, but they always just walk in anyway. When she turns her head toward me, it looks like she's seen a ghost.

My first thought is that Pit Bull escaped from jail and is here to kill us, but then Erika wouldn't have asked if I knew the person. My second thought is that someone's coming to take me to jail because, technically, I didn't complete my six-month sentence at Serenity

Ranch. My third thought…actually, I don't have time for another thought because when Erika steps aside, I see my father standing in the doorway.

"Hello Jake," he says, not sure whether he should enter the room. "I hope it's not too late to pay you a visit."

I don't usually find speaking difficult, but it happens again—my brain is working, but my mouth won't move. My father takes this as an invitation and steps inside.

He looks different than I remember him—thinner, older, weaker. Maybe it's just the light, but he's not the same person I wanted to kill six months ago.

"Maybe I should go get some coffee," Erika says, "would either of you like some?"

"No, but thank you. That's very kind of you," my father says, extending his hand. "You must be Erika."

"How do you know my name," she asks, still on edge about letting him in my room.

"I read your article. It was a fascinating story, and, I must say, your journalism skills are top-notch. If you ever want to explore work in advertising, let me know. I could use someone like you on my team."

"Oh, no," Erica replies, "I like being a reporter. It's where all the action is."

"Judging from your article, I would agree with you. But, unfortunately, not everyone makes as good of an undercover reporter as you."

"Well, it has its perks," she says, looking at me.

I haven't said a word, and I'm feeling more uncomfortable as each second passes. I feel anxiety building inside of me, and I feel like I'm going to panic any second.

There isn't a day that I don't think about what I'd say to my father if he were standing in front of me. It's usually an entire sentence of four-letter words.

"Is that how you heard I was here?" I ask, wondering what he thought when he saw my name in the newspaper.

"No. I have a friend on the hospital board, and he called me the day you came in."

"And it's taken you this long to come and see me?"

My father chuckles. This is how most of our conversations begin.

"Actually, I've come by several times in the last couple of weeks," he says. "I didn't want to burden Erika, so I just stood outside and looked in on you through the window. My friend called me yesterday and told me you'd regained consciousness. First, however, I had to check with your doctor to see if you could have visitors."

"Why did you come?" I ask bluntly.

He pauses for a moment and then turns to Erika, "You know, on second thought, I'd love a cup of coffee. Black, no sugar," he says, thanking her as she leaves the room.

When we're alone and the door is shut, he looks at me and sighs. "I'm here because it's time we talked, Jake. I want to get some things out in the open to help us move on with our lives. I've been seeing a psychiatrist for months, and I've been able to make some progress."

"Progress toward what? Being the world's worst father?"

"I know, Jake, that's the path I was on for a very long time, but today is a new day, and I came to make amends with you. I'm trying to get my personal affairs in order before it's too late."

"Too late for what?" I ask, waiting to see how he turns this on me.

"I'm dying," he says. "I've got cancer."

"Cancer?"

"Yes, my doctors performed a CT scan and found a tumor in my limbic system. The doctor ordered a biopsy, and we found out it is malignant, meaning that it's still growing."

"W-What are they doing about it?"

"There's not much they can do," he says, "it's inoperable."

"They can't take it out?"

"The tumor formed around a major artery in my brain. The surgeon believes that if they try to remove it, there's a good chance I'll bleed out on the operating table."

"So, they're not doing anything for you? Chemotherapy? Radiation? Medication? Nothing?"

I can't believe I'm having this conversation with the person I hate most in this world, except for Pit Bull. I'd typically be quite pleased to hear my father was dying and no one can save him, but I'm not.

"We've tried all that and more, but the tumor is still metastasizing. It's just a matter of time now before it cuts off the blood circulation to my brain, and I die."

"That's impossible!" I argue. "There's got to be something more they can do."

"Jake, it's okay. I've accepted it. I'm at peace with it. I've come to make my amends with you and say goodbye."

"Goodbye?" I ask, still not believing what he's telling me. "How bad is it?"

He chuckles again, but I can tell now that he's scared. "It's bad, Jake—really bad."

"How much time do you have left?"

"No one knows," he says quietly. "It's probably better that way because I can't procrastinate some of the things I need to do before I go."

"Like what? Show up here and ask me to forgive you? Is that what you expect to happen?"

"I just want to tell you that I've been sick for a very long time. The doctors said this tumor affects my emotional responses and behavior. Apparently, it's been there for several years but just started growing again recently."

"Emotional responses? Is this why you blame me for Nate's death?"

"I don't blame you for Nate's death, Jake. I blame myself, but I haven't been acting rationally when it comes to conveying my emotions. I hadn't realized how my isolation from you and your mother affected you. I didn't even realize what I was doing was wrong."

"Did you have this tumor when I was in high school?"

"The doctors say this has been around for ten to twelve years. They don't know why it stopped growing for a while and then started again recently."

"Did this tumor have something to do with…" I don't even want to say it.

His eyes close, and his head drops to his chest. "Most likely, Jake. I know it doesn't excuse what I did, but you have to believe me—I've been very sick for a very long time."

"But how have you been so successful with your company if you were sick all this time?"

"I don't know. I guess because the tumor didn't affect that part of my brain—just the part that deals with emotions and behavior."

As I try to comprehend what my father is telling me, my own brain feels like it isn't working right. I'm angry, sad, and confused, all at the same time.

"I just want you to know, Jake, that I'm sorry." He continues, expecting me to call security any second and throw him out. "I'm sorry for letting you think I thought you were somehow responsible for your bother drowning. I'm sorry for things that happened when I wasn't in control of myself. I'm sorry I passed genes on to you that preconditioned you to addiction…. I'm sorry I've been the world's worst father."

Tears are streaming down my father's face as he stands at the foot of my hospital bed. Tears cascade down my cheeks as well. I feel like I'm in a dream and that I'll wake up any second, but I know I'm not asleep.

He moves closer to my bed and puts his hand on my good foot. "Is there any way you can find it in your heart to forgive me, son?"

*****

When Erika returns with the coffee, she's surprised that my father is sitting next to my bed. She's even more surprised that we're not yelling or trying to kill each other.

As difficult as it may be, I know what I have to do. I have to forgive my father—not just because he's dying—people die every day. It's that if I don't make amends with my father, I'll never stay sober. Forgiving him is the only way I can let go and let God heal our wounds.

Erika checks on us and understands that this is going to be a long conversation. Rather than pretend she's not listening or wandering the halls, she says that she's going to a laundromat down the street to wash some clothes. I get a new hospital gown every day; I didn't even realize she was running low on clothes.

"No, you don't need to do that," my father says, "I'll send someone to collect your things and have them dry cleaned."

Erika looks at the pants she's wearing—the same ones she shoveled horse poop in for four months—and laughs. "Thank you, Mr. Coleman, but I'm fine. In fact, I'm just going to throw some things in the wash cycle and go for a run. I've always wanted to tour the University of Washington campus. What better way than on a run?

"But it's dark outside," my father argues. "You're not scared of getting hurt or mugged?"

Erika and I look at each other and laugh. I don't know that anything could scare either of us ever again. And I'd certainly like to meet the guy who thinks he could take Erika. I've seen her wrestle a steer to the ground, which is twice as dangerous as any night prowler on the UW campus.

"How's your ankle?" I ask.

"The doctor said it's looking good. It was just a sprain. I don't break as easily as you."

"Oh, okay, then," I say, sticking my tongue out at her. "Please be careful."

Once she's packed up some things and headed out, my father tells me that my mother has been getting help as well.

"Remember that treatment center you went to down in Malibu? I think its name is New Life."

"Mom checked into *New Life*?"

"Yes, she's been there for about eight weeks now, and she's doing really well."

"No kidding?" I ask, trying to imagine my mother sitting in a group therapy session with Mel Gibson and Johnny Depp.

"She's carried a lot of baggage around," my father says, "I hope she can leave a few suitcases and handbags behind, but more importantly, I pray she can learn to forgive herself. That seems to be the hardest part."

"Do you think I could talk to her sometime?" I ask.

"I think she would love that. I'll set it up. I'd really appreciate it if you could look in on her from time to time when I'm gone."

"Of course. We've got a lot of catching up to do. We need to spend some time together."

"Thank you, Jake," he says, putting his arms around me the best he can with my casts, cords, and IVs. "You have no idea how happy you've made me today. I'd trade every penny I have for another day on this earth with you and your brother."

Our embrace lasts for several minutes, both of us crying almost to the point of sobbing. People say never let anyone see you cry, but I've lived my entire life trying to hide my emotions. So it feels liberating to let the tears fall where they fall. It bathes my soul in peace.

"Hey, Dad? How about if we go fishing when I get out of here?"

"Flyfishing?" he asks, remembering the feel of a well-weighted flyrod in his hand.

"Of course. I know a great river we could fish this time of year."

"I'd love to, son, more than you will ever know."

EPILOGUE

The last rays of sunshine hang in the evening sky the way fog clings to the ground on cold winter mornings. It's late in the evening, and it won't be long before the twilight reclaims the ground it surrendered in the tug-of-war between night and day.

I tug on the horse's reins, but he knows the way and ignores me, similar to how Erika ignores me when I tell her how to wear her hair. It's only another 200 yards before we'll crest the hill that overlooks the lodge, the lake, and our legacy—hers and mine.

The valley hasn't changed much, but we have, and this valley has a lot to do with that. We've been living here for ten years, and I cannot imagine calling any other place home.

As my horse carries me over the horizon, I see her picking wildflowers that grow near the barn. They are her favorite color, the color of the ocean, a deep azure blue that will look spectacular in a vase next to our bed.

At her side is our son, Seth, named after a good friend whose life was cut short by an insidious drug. He is almost five now, and he loves to ride with Erika and me in the evenings, but tonight I needed to be alone.

Today marks ten years since my father passed away from cancer. He lived only four months from when I learned about his illness, and they were some of the best days of my life—hopefully, his as well.

He died at home, in his sleep, and I was grateful that his suffering ended, but I was also heartbroken that we didn't have more time to spend with one another.

He wanted me to take over as CEO of Coleman Pharmaceutical Laboratories, but that was never something I wanted to do. The board of trustees runs the company and does a much better job than I could ever do. Furthermore, CPL is a company that makes drugs, and I don't want any part of it.

Instead, my father bought Serenity Ranch and gave it to me. We still call it by that name because, well, it's where I feel most at peace. It's still a working cattle ranch for drug addicts and alcoholics who come here to learn how to live sober lives. As a result, hundreds of young men and women have walked out of here with a chance to make a fresh start—and all of them were here by choice.

I don't recall what happened to Pit Bull or Vanessa, except I know both were doing time in state prison after they were found guilty of murder and conspiracy to commit murder, respectively. I just didn't want to rent out any more space to them in my head.

Erika and I did train for and run a marathon together. We ran the Seattle marathon because my mother wanted to be there to see us finish. Unfortunately, her health isn't great, so she doesn't leave the house very often. She loves her grandson, though, so we try to visit her as often as possible.

I don't think she'll be around much longer, but we believe families can be together, even after death. That knowledge alone brings me great peace, and I can hardly wait for that reunion.

Drew and Todd run the ranch, for the most part. Drew is responsible for the cattle operation while Todd takes care of the treatment side of the ranch. I stay out of their way as much as possible, but that doesn't mean I don't attend every support group meeting we hold.

Kris came and visited me while I was recovering in the hospital. He read Erika's article and said he had to see me with his own eyes and make sure I was okay. Kris lived another seven years and came up to the ranch quite often. When he died, there were no less than two thousand people at his funeral. I was just one of the many addicts and alcoholics he helped in his 39 years of sobriety. Without him, I wouldn't be here today.

I spent the morning flyfishing on the Yakima River, and although I came home empty-handed, it was still a wonderful day. I caught three good-sized rainbows, but I'm a "catch and release" fisherman because I think everything, and everyone, deserves another chance—I know I am blessed to have had many chances in my own life.

The last time I fished with my father was right before he died. I'd only been out of the hospital a couple of months, but the physical therapy helped me heal much faster than anyone anticipated. I didn't wade very far into the river that day, but that wasn't because I was too weak or that I was afraid of the water, I just didn't want to leave my father's side.

On the anniversary of his death, Erika and I went to the spot in the river where Nate drowned and scattered my father's ashes. I think he wanted me to do that because he considered the Yakima River to be healing waters and because he loved to flyfish and be with his sons.

I still fish that spot of the river a couple of times each year, especially when I get sad or want to spend time with God. When I go there, I like to believe that my father and Nate are right there with me, casting our lines and waiting for a bite.

Apart from Serenity Ranch, that river is my favorite place to be. It reminds me each time I visit that, although I'm still and addict—I'm a recovering addict with ten years sobriety.

ABOUT THE AUTHOR

Jason A. Densley is a native of Idaho Falls, Idaho, and a retired Lieutenant Colonel from the United States Air Force. He holds a B.S. degree in Psychology from the University of Utah, a Master of Law degree from California Southern University, and a Master of Military Operational Arts and Sciences from The Air University. Jason enjoys paragliding, scuba diving, motorcycles, running marathons, and competing in triathlons. Jason is married to the former Melinda McAllister from Dothan, Alabama, and has four children, Chandler, Logan, Madison, and Noah.

Made in the USA
Columbia, SC
24 December 2021